To Christine [signature]

Forever Ink

A Montgomery Ink Novella

CARRIE ANN RYAN

Author Highlights

Praise for Carrie Ann Ryan...

"Carrie Ann Ryan knows how to pull your heartstrings and make your pulse pound! Her wonderful Redwood Pack series will draw you in and keep you reading long into the night. I can't wait to see what comes next with the new generation, the Talons. Keep them coming, Carrie Ann!" –Lara Adrian, New York Times bestselling author of CRAVE THE NIGHT

"With snarky humor, sizzling love scenes, and brilliant, imaginative worldbuilding, The Dante's Circle series reads as if Carrie Ann Ryan peeked at my personal wish list!" – NYT Bestselling Author, Larissa Ione

"Carrie Ann Ryan writes sexy shifters in a world full of passionate happily-ever-afters." – *New York Times* Bestselling Author Vivian Arend

"Carrie Ann's books are sexy with characters you can't help but love from page one. They are heat and heart blended to perfection." *New York Times* Bestselling Author Jayne Rylon

Carrie Ann Ryan's books are wickedly funny and deliciously hot, with plenty of twists to keep you guessing. They'll keep you up all night!" USA Today Bestselling Author Cari Quinn

"Once again, Carrie Ann Ryan knocks the Dante's Circle series out of the park. The queen of hot, sexy, enthralling paranormal romance, Carrie Ann is an author not to miss!" *New York Times* bestselling Author Marie Harte

Praise for the Redwood Pack Series...

"You will not be disappointed in the Redwood Pack." *Books-n-Kisses*

"I was so completely immersed in this story that I felt what the characters felt. BLOWN AWAY." *Delphina's Book Reviews.*

"I love all the wolves in the Redwood Pack and eagerly anticipate all the brothers' stories." *The Book Vixen*

"Shifter romances are a dime a dozen, but good ones aren't as plentiful as one would think. This is one of the goods one." *Book Binge*

"With the hints of things to come for the Redwoods, I can't wait to read the next book!" *Scorching Book Reviews*

"Ryan outdid herself on this book." *The Romance Reviews*

Praise for the Dante's Circle Series...

"This author better write the next books quickly or I will Occupy Her Lawn until she releases more! Pure romance enjoyment here. Now go put this on your TBR pile—shoo!" *The Book Vixen*

"I, for one, will definitely be following the series to see what happens to the seven." *Cocktails & Books*

"The world of Dante's Circle series is enthralling and with each book gets deeper and deeper as does Carrie Ann's writing." Literal Addiction

Praise for the Montgomery Ink Series...

"Shea and Shep are so cute together and really offset each other in a brilliant way. " *Literal Addiction*

"This was a very quick and spicy read. I really enjoyed reading about Sassy, Rafe & Ian. I really hope there will be more of these three in the future." *Books n Kisses*

Praise for the Holiday, Montana Series...

"Charmed Spirits was a solid first book in this new series and I'm looking forward to seeing where it goes." *RR@H Novel Thoughts & Book Thoughts*

"If you're looking for a light book full of magic, love and hot little scenes on various objects, then this book is for you! You'll soon find that tables are no longer for eating meals of the food variety ... Bon appétit!" *Under the Covers*

"The book was well written and had the perfect setting the steamy bits where really really hot and the story one of sweet romance. Well done Carrie" *Bitten by Love Reviews*

Forever Ink

Callie Masters loves ink. After finally getting her own chair in Montgomery Ink, she's ready to start being a full time artist, rather than only an apprentice. When Austin, her former boss, gives her one very broody man as her first client, she jumps at the chance to make him hers—in and out of the shop.

Morgan McAllister is old money, old connections, and recently has been feeling just old. When he goes in to get his full back piece done after years of putting it off, the bright-eyed woman with the sly smile catches his eye. Between her age, attitude, and views on life, he knows she's all wrong for him, but that doesn't mean she'll keep out of his thoughts.

When life throws them together after a few close calls, Morgan and Callie will have to trust in themselves and what their relationship will mean. Between conniving family members, blondes with too much time on their hands, and their own misgivings, trust in the bedroom and out of it won't come easy.

CHAPTER ONE

Being bent over a table for long hours was only one of the perks in being Callie Masters. No, really...the ache that came from that position felt like nothing else. Since being bent over in just that way came from her inking a new client *on her own* with a brilliant—if she did say so herself—tattoo, she couldn't wait for the ache again. In fact, if she was reading her boss right, she might just be in for more soon.

Today was going to be a kickass day. Callie did a little hip shake around the office, humming to herself. When her hands went up into the air, she closed her eyes, swaying to music only she could hear. She danced to the beat in her head, getting herself in the mindset to work. That wasn't difficult since she freaking *loved* her job. *I'm doing what I always dreamed of doing—and I get* paid *for it. How lucky is that?* She was twenty-five and knew she was well on her way to actually having a career bringing art, happiness, and memories to those who asked for it.

Being an apprentice to Austin Montgomery, the co-owner of Montgomery Ink, was a dream come true for some tattoo artists, and she was the one who held the coveted spot. Austin had only apprenticed one other before her, and that had been a few years before she'd come to the shop in search of a new life. She did another hip shake and turned on her heel twice. Her earrings tapped against her jaw as she wiggled around.

Yes, she'd had just a bit too much coffee. She couldn't help it though since her favorite place, Taboo, had a side entrance to the shop. Plus, her friend Hailey owned and operated it. Callie felt it was her duty to support the local businesses.

She shook her butt again.

Maybe she should lay off the caffeine. Just a bit.

"Seriously? Dancing alone in the office without any music is weird. Even for you."

Sloane, her friend and co-worker, said it with a smile, but Callie still blushed right up to the roots of her black and red hair. She blinked up at the big bald man who didn't smile as often as he should. He towered over her but she knew he was a big softie.

Okay, so he could probably crush someone's head with his bare hands, but he was like her big brother.

Still, he didn't have to make fun of her.

"I was alone. I'm allowed to dance if I want to."

Sloane snorted. "Sure you can, sweetie. And when I walk in on you, I'm going to call you crazy. But we still love you."

She punched him in the stomach and winced at the pain in her hand. Did all the men in Montgomery Ink bulk up to work here? She felt so puny next to them. Most girls would love that, and she probably would too if she didn't work day in and day out with them. They all treated her like she was their little sister. It didn't bother her much considering she felt the same way relationship-wise, but it would be nice if a man gave her a passing glance once in a while.

Whoa. Where had that come from? Apparently, coming down from a caffeine high led one down the path of loneliness, self-doubt and self-pity. Best to head that off at the pass and get more caffeine.

Her body begged for the stuff and she grinned. Yep, coffee could fix anything.

"How's your hand?" Sloane asked, bringing her out of her coffee fixation.

She waved it in the air, then stretched her fingers. "Fine, but next time at least try to make it look like I could hurt you. Okay?"

His lips twitched and he patted her on the head. See? There was no way she'd find him attractive, not when he made her feel like she was his baby sister. Not that there was anything wrong with that. She loved her Montgomery Ink family.

She just needed to get laid.

Well then, more caffeine and new avenues of thought were needed.

Stat.

"What is going on in that head of yours?" Sloane asked as he moved around her. He shuffled through a few blank notebooks before finding one that fit his tastes, then did the same with the pencils.

"Nothing." She cursed. "I mean, nothing important. I think I just need a chai or something." She shuffled her feet, not knowing what was wrong with her. She'd been antsy for a while now and she couldn't figure it out. Yes, everything was going great—job, friends, and life in general— and she couldn't complain, but for some reason, she felt as if she were on the precipice of something...waiting for something she couldn't quite name. It was as if she were waiting on the sidelines for something to happen.

And she *hated* waiting.

Callie preferred action. If she hadn't gone for what she wanted in the first place, she wouldn't be where she was today.

It wasn't like she could control that emotion though, so she needed to push it aside and actually get to work.

"What are you going to draw today?" she asked Sloane when he didn't comment on her drink preference. He knew she was a caffeine addict and there was no changing her.

Sloane looked at her briefly out of the corner of his eye before running his hand over the blank page. She loved watching her artists work. They had a system, a way that was unique to each of them. And yes, she did consider them *her* artists. One day, she might even have a chair and a station of her own. One day.

"There's a guy coming in tomorrow for a consult, ex-military." An odd expression passed over his face, and she held back the urge to comfort him. She knew Sloane was also ex-military, but he never talked about it and she never pushed him. She knew better than that. "He said over the phone he wanted a hawk on his back so I'm going to get him a few samples."

Callie nodded, her throat closing up. "And you want this one to be special," she said quietly.

Sloane gave her a brief nod, then got back to work, his attention on the pad in front of him—or maybe in the past she and her friends could never quite reach.

She backed out of the office quietly, grabbing her own notepad, pencil, and wallet on the way. She loved her brothers- and sister-in-ink so much sometimes that it hurt. She wanted to fix all of them but it wasn't her place.

"Hey, you going to Hailey's?" Austin asked from his stool. He had one hand on a beefy dude in front of him and a tattoo gun in the other. Curious, she walked over to them to admire his work.

She held back a happy sigh at the look of the iguana wrapping itself around the man's upper arm. Austin was a genius when it came to shading and coloring. He was working on the different shades of green, blending them in so well it looked like a photo, rather than ink on skin.

"Callie?"

"What? Oh yeah, I'm going to Hailey's. You want something?"

"A small iced coffee would be great. I need a boost." He glanced at his client. "You want a smoothie or juice from there? We have some things in the fridge, but if Callie is going next door, might as well get something better."

His client gave Callie his order—a large strawberry smoothie—and she left the two of them to it. When she got back, she'd either sit with Austin and watch him work, or maybe take a walk. She was at the point where Austin and his sister Maya let her work on small tattoos with their supervision. Anything that took less than an hour was fair game and she loved it. She also knew she was ready for the next step, at least she felt like it, and she hoped Austin felt the same way.

Callie walked through the side door into Taboo, Hailey's café and inhaled the rich aroma of soup, fresh coffee, and baked goods. Her mouth watered and she figured she should probably get a small snack while she was there. Caffeine only did so much.

Hailey stood behind the counter, talking to one of her regulars. Her friend's bleach blonde bob shined under the lights, not a hair out of place. Callie didn't know how the other woman did it. She looked perfect even after a long day of working with food, humidity, and customers who had long days as well.

Callie ran a hand through her black and red hair, knowing it probably looked like she'd just rolled out of bed. She'd used the flat iron over it that morning, but Denver was oddly humid that day. Considering the city air usually sucked the moisture right out of her skin most days, that was saying something.

"Stop playing with your hair. You look beautiful. As always. Lucky bitch." Hailey winked, then came over to Callie. "Sit down and tell me what you need."

"A man?" she blurted, then shut her eyes. Damn. Totally not what she meant to say.

Hailey threw her head back and laughed. "It's about time you said that, although I don't know if you need a man so much as to get laid."

The other customer at the counter sputtered his coffee and Callie laughed, turning to him. "She meant that I don't need a man in my life, just an orgasm. I'm not a lesbian. Well, I made out with a couple girls when I was, like, nineteen, but that was just experimenting. It's good to make sure you're sure about what you want, you know?"

The man blushed hard, put money on the counter, and scurried away.

Hailey laughed beside her. "If I didn't know that man has probably heard worse coming in

8

here and listening to Maya talk, I'd get angry with you for scaring away business."

Callie rolled her eyes. "What? He was listening in to you talking about me getting laid. I just wanted to clarify."

"You're a dork, but I love you. Now, tell me what you want caffeine and food wise since I can't help you with the getting laid thing."

"Shame," Callie teased.

Hailey tapped her fingers on the counter. "You know I'm swoon-worthy, but I'm not what you need. Nor are you what I want." Her eyes drifted over to Montgomery Ink and Callie held back a retort. There were secrets friends kept for one another. Longing, unrequited love, and lust were just parts of it.

"I want an iced chai, Austin wants a small iced coffee, his client wants a large strawberry smoothie, and I think I'll take a fruit salad too since I need sustenance."

Hailey nodded, then turned back to start working on Callie's order. "What about Sloane?" Hailey asked casually. Too casually.

Callie sighed. She couldn't fix her friends' problems even if she desperately wanted to. "He's working on a project that's probably going to take a lot out of him. I didn't want to bother him by asking for his drink order when he was so focused."

Hailey shook her head, mumbling to herself. "I'll get him his energy shake and make him a cup of soup." She looked over her shoulder. "Make sure he eats it. Okay?"

Callie nodded, knowing Hailey wanted to take care of Sloane even if she couldn't do it personally. There was only so much she could do, and since Callie was sure she didn't know the whole of it, she wouldn't interfere. It wasn't her place.

Hailey put the food in a bag, and the cups in a container when she was finished. "You need help getting everything over there?"

Callie shook her head. "No, I've got this. If there was another drink order, then I'd need help, but Maya is off today so we're good."

"She out with Jake again?"

Callie snorted. "Yep. It's her day off so she's off doing something with Jake. They're just friends though, Hailey. I'm pretty sure they've never slept together since I don't get those vibes."

"You can't *just* be friends with a man like that."

"Maybe, maybe not. I'm friends with him. In fact, I'm friends with the whole crew, and I haven't slept with any of them."

Hailey sighed. "Yeah, but you work with them and they treat you like a sister. Jake doesn't treat Maya like a sister."

"No, he treats her like one of the guys. I honestly think they're good as friends. Plus she gets enough shit about it that I don't want to tease her."

Hailey threw her head back and laughed. "Honey, you tease her about sleeping with him all the time. You even call her out on it in public and joke about it. She jokes right back, so it's just the way the two of you work."

Callie blushed. That was true. Maya scared most people since she was brash, had more ink than some deemed lady-like, and spoke her mind. She used to intimidate Callie too, but then Callie had seen beneath the gruff exterior into the woman that cared for those she loved with all her heart. Now the two of them joked around and Jake was just more fodder. If Callie had ever caught a glimpse of pain in the other woman's eyes, she'd never do it, but Maya took it in stride and teased right back.

"I'll see you later, hon. Don't work too hard."

"I never do," Hailey lied.

Callie rolled her eyes, then made her way back into the shop. She dropped off Sloane's soup and drink in the office. He didn't acknowledge her, his focus on the drawing in front of him. She didn't sneak a peek though, since she didn't want to pry, but she wanted to.

"Eat this or I'll sic Hailey on you," she said softly.

Sloane froze and slowly looked over to the soup. "Thanks," he said gruffly, then went back to work.

Shit. Maybe mentioning Hailey's name while he was in the zone wasn't the best thing to do, but she couldn't take it back now. She went back out into the shop and handed Austin his drink while setting his client's smoothie in front of him.

"So how goes things?" she asked, taking a sip of her chai. Yummy cinnamon goodness.

The client mumbled something and she snuck a look at Austin.

"We're almost done, Geoff is just in the zone." Austin stopped and looked over at his client's face. "You still good, bro?"

"Yeah, it doesn't hurt, but the vibrating is getting to me."

Austin nodded and got back to work. The buzz of the needle calmed Callie at the same time as it excited her. The paradox was what made her a tattoo artist. She loved the idea of creating something new while knowing the act itself was something she could dive deep into.

"Getting close. I'm just shading the last bit now then we'll cover you up. I know after a while the sound can be too much."

"Thanks," Geoff mumbled, his eyes closed.

"Anything you want me to do?" Callie asked as Austin worked.

Austin tilted his head toward the front of the shop. "We have a walk in sitting in the chairs looking at the books. Then later we have a consult that I want you to be part of. From what the girl said she wanted, you should be able to handle it yourself."

Callie beamed, her fingers tapping along her thigh. She couldn't wait to get started, but doing another dance probably wouldn't show off the calm, cool, and collected persona most badass tattoo artists radiated.

"What's the consult?" she asked, eager to start working on the girl's tattoo even though she knew she should get all the information first.

"A friend of mine from while back. You'll see. I think you'll be intrigued."

Callie's brow raised at that cryptic comment, then sucked back more of her chai. "Okay, then. Where do you want me to work?" Since she wasn't a full time tattoo artist, she didn't have a station of her own. She had her own kit and tools that she's acquired over time, but unlike the others, she didn't have a chair and area of her own. She bounced around from station to station, usually sharing space so she could learn and be watched over as she did so. It didn't bother her since most people had to work that way when they first started and she honestly learned a lot from just having someone there to help her if needed.

Austin looked up from Geoff's arm. "Go take the empty one near Sloane. You should be done with what the girl wants by the time Morgan gets here."

Her body stiffened at the mention of an empty station. That was new.

"Morgan?" she asked, trying to sound casual about what his other words meant.

"My friend with the consult." Austin grinned. "And yeah, Callie. Take the extra station. We cleared it out for you last night."

Callie froze, her eyes filling. "What?"

Austin, cursed, then patted Geoff's back. "Give me a sec."

"Sure thing. If you're about do to what I think you're about to do, then I'm glad I'm here to witness it."

Callie swallowed hard, her gaze going from Austin, to Geoff, to the empty station, then back to Austin. "What do you mean?"

"You're ready for your own space, hon," Austin said softly. "You've been ready for awhile, but Maya and I wanted to be sure the shop was ready too. Since Tommy moved away when his wife got stationed in Texas last week, we've opened up a space. So it's yours. We'll talk business and what it all means when Maya gets back, but welcome to the family. You're one of us."

Callie threw her arms around Austin's neck, crying softly. "Oh thank you so much. Thank you, thank you, thank you."

Austin patted her back and set her down. "You're good at what you do. So go work on the star for that girl over there and then we can work with Morgan together."

She nodded, a bit dazed, then kissed Austin on the cheek. "Thank you."

"Putting moves on my man?" Sierra teased as she walked in.

Callie blushed then stepped back from Austin. "He just told me I get my own station, so I was just saying thanks. He's all yours."

Sierra beamed and hugged her tight. Callie closed her eyes, letting her family in everything but blood celebrate with her. "I'm so proud of you." She looked over at Austin. "Maya's going to be pissed you didn't wait for her."

Austin shrugged. "Whatever. I want Callie to work with Morgan and Maya isn't here. She'll get over it."

Callie winced. "I so don't want to be here when you're telling her that."

"Whatever," Austin mumbled, his attention on his work.

"It's good to see you," Callie said to Sierra.

"You too, honey. I'm just stopping in to say hi on my way out to see another boutique in the area."

Callie raised a brow. "Problems?" Sierra owned Eden, a new boutique across the street. That's how she and Austin had met.

"Problems? Oh no. Not at all. I just like to know what the other shops are selling. It's good to know your rivals."

Callie grinned. "Oh, good. Have fun and let me know how it goes."

"Will do and congratulations, honey."

"Thank you!" Callie bounced her way to the girl sitting in the waiting room, trying to act causal and totally failing. Whatever, she was a full-fledged tattoo artist now. With a station and everything. She could act perky and her age if she wanted.

"Hi, I'm Callie and I'll be your artist today." *Yay*. "Come on over to my station and we'll talk stars." *Her* station. Yay again.

The girl smiled at her. "I'm Jessica. It's nice to meet you."

Callie led Jessica over to her new station and talked stars and placement. Austin was right; this would be a super easy first tattoo on her own. The girl wanted it on the inside of her wrist, no bigger than a fingernail. Plus she only wanted the outline and no fill.

"Let me get my things and then we can get started," Callie said then headed back to the office to get her kit.

By the time she got everything ready and started sketching in front of Jessica, she was jazzed and ready to start inking. She stenciled the star on the girl's wrist, got approval, and started tattooing. The buzz went straight to her bones and she grinned.

God, she loved her job.

Jessica didn't flinch as Callie worked. It really depended on the person and location if someone was going to move around a lot during a session. This girl didn't seem too bothered by the needle and Callie counted herself grateful. A perfect client and tattoo for her first job all on her own. Sure, she'd done tattoos before, but never on her own. Never in a station she could make *hers*. Austin, Sloane, Maya and the others would be there if she needed them, but right then, she was all on her own.

And oh my, didn't that sound amazing?

By the time she finished up the paperwork and said goodbye to Jessica, Austin was already done with another consult after Geoff had left. Sloane was at his station, working on a leg piece that she'd want to get a look at later and they had a nice flow to the room. Not too busy, yet enough people to make her feel like she was in the right place.

The hairs on the back of her neck tingled and she shivered. She turned toward the door and blinked once. Twice.

The sexiest man she'd ever seen in her life stood in the doorway.

No, stood wasn't a good word, not with the way his presence filled the shop. Dear Lord, was she panting? His broad shoulders were encased in a suit that had to cost more than her rent, but she didn't care about that. His thick chest tapered into a trim waist and strong thighs. Just the thought of those thighs made her clench her own. He had his hands fisted at his sides, and oh God, those hands. Large, thick, and they looked so out of place compared to his classy suit. It looked as if he actually *used* his hands rather than merely sitting behind a desk as his attire suggested.

She let her gaze rake over his body and settle on his face. His attention was focused in front of him so she got his profile. He'd clenched his jaw, but damn, he looked amazing. He had to be in his late thirties or early forties. He had one of the expensive haircuts that made his dark brown strands look like they were perfectly manicured. With the way his hair had gone silver on his sideburns, it made him look even more dangerous.

He might be older her than her, but her hormones didn't care. No, they screamed 'fuck yeah, let's ride'. Her nipples tightened and she thanked God she'd worn a bra that morning. Talk about embarrassing if that was the first thing he'd see.

He turned toward her and she sucked in a breath. Piercing blue eyes stared back at her, studying her like they would something they didn't quite understand.

Not something she was unfamiliar with.

She wanted this man. Now. Later. More than once.

"Morgan, glad you made it," Austin said as he walked up to the man with the sexy eyes. He held out a hand and Morgan clasped it.

"Thanks for sparing the time for me," Morgan said, his voice low, gruff. So deep that it vibrated straight to her pussy.

Damn. This was Morgan. The man Austin wanted her to ink. It wouldn't do well for her to lust after him. Sure, Austin had ended up engaged to Sierra after a consult, but sleeping with clients wasn't the best way to start a career.

Her libido cursed at her and she pushed it aside. She'd just look from afar...even as she put her hands on him in a professional sense.

"Callie."

She shook her head and looked up at the men again. It seemed they'd been trying to get her attention and she'd been off in her own dirty thoughts.

"Sorry, I was woolgathering."

Austin gave her a curious look then motioned for her to come over. "Morgan, this is Callie Masters. Callie, this is one of my old friends, Morgan McAllister. From what you said you wanted Morgan, I really think Callie is going to do a great job on your ink."

Morgan frowned. "Has she been tattooing long? I thought I'd come in and get you to work on me, not a new student."

Callie bit back the frustration at the fact he talked about her like she wasn't even there. "I'm experienced, Mr. McAllister. Don't worry, I won't screw up your tattoo."

"Yeah, Morgan. She's an amazing artist and exquisite with color. You're going to be in good hands."

Morgan narrowed his eyes. "If you say so."

"He does," Callie bit back. Normally she was a little more gracious when it came to clients. It wasn't as if she'd been immune to people thinking she couldn't cut it before. But he'd heated her up quickly then just as fast, cooled her down.

She might want to fuck him, or at least might have *wanted*—past tense—but now she wanted to prove to him she was good enough. He was way too rigid for her and that 'student' comment told her he thought she was too young.

Austin looked between the two of them then met her gaze. She nodded, telling him with her eyes that she could handle it. Later, when Morgan wasn't there, she'd tell Austin how she felt. He seemed to understand, then took a step back.

"Okay then. I'll let the two of you work together." He squeezed Morgan's shoulder. "I wouldn't put you into hands I didn't trust with all my heart. Got me?"

Morgan nodded, but didn't lose the frown. Whatever, she'd prove to him—and herself—she could do this.

She led him to her new station and gestured for him to sit down. He did so, but didn't lose the suit jacket, that rigidness never leaving his body.

"What is it you wanted?" she asked, trying to keep her voice warm. She wouldn't let this guy rock her. She'd been through worse; she could do this.

"A full back piece that goes down the back of my arms, but also is easily covered up in a suit."

Well damn. That was big. *Really* big.

"What do you want it of?"

He met her eyes. "A phoenix."

A symbol for rebirth. For change.

She could do this. Her fingers itched to start sketching. Oh damn, she couldn't wait to ink this on his body.

She smiled then. "That's something we can do, Mr. McAllister. Don't you worry, you're in good hands."

He raised a brow, but she didn't blush. She'd give him the best tattoo of her life and then she'd let him walk away. Morgan McAllister and all his sexiness weren't for her, but she'd show him what she could do with her ink.

She was Callie Masters. Kickass tattoo artist.

CHAPTER TWO

Morgan McAllister was going to hell. There could be no other result for his very, very impure thoughts. The desires running through his veins didn't help things either. Dear God, he'd wanted to flip Callie over and pump into her until they were both panting and sweaty. He could practically feel her cunt gripping his cock, squeezing him until he shook in sweet agony.

He'd wanted to tie her up, have her beg him to fuck her, then spank her for that dirty mouth of hers. He'd slide his cock in and out of her mouth, watching his length get wetter and wetter as he fucked her face.

Jesus. That wasn't going to happen.

Now he had a hard-on and had to think past what he wanted to do with his little tattoo artist.

His.

Damn it, no. She wasn't his. Not only was she someone who would be working with him on a tattoo—and, therefore, off limits—she had to be a good fifteen years or more younger than him. He would be cradle robbing at that point. There were only so many 'dirty old man' taunts he could take. Sure, he was only forty, but hell, that was too damn old to be having such thoughts about the girl who worked for Austin.

While he'd been in the shop, he held back his tongue so he wouldn't ask his friend the important questions.

How old was she?

Was she single?

Did he know if she liked to be tied up?

And the question only she could answer: Would she kneel at his feet, and wait for his command?

Well, that last one he had a feeling was a steady yes. She had that spark in her eyes that spoke of defiance when he'd spoken about her as if she hadn't been in the room, but she was also a submissive. Something about her made him want to grasp the back of her neck and watch her relax, watch her shoulders fall as she came to him willingly.

She was short in stature, slender, and she would fit perfectly against his side. Her hair was a reddish color with black stripes, or maybe it had been the other way around. Either way, it looked like a hairstyle some punk kid would wear, but it suited her perfectly. She'd straightened it so it fell around her face and down her shoulders. He could easily see it brushing his chest as she bent over him, taking his cock deep inside her cunt.

Her breasts would easily fit in his hands. They looked like they were tight and firm, high, and sufficiently plump. Her nipples had pressed through her bra just enough that he could see the outline of those suckable berries. He wanted to nip at them, put them in clamps, and suck around her tits until she came hard on his hand. His three or four fingers would fuck her hard and find her G-spot so she would fill his palm with her orgasm. He wanted her on her knees in front of him so she could take him in her mouth.

He wanted to cherish her.

His cock throbbed, and he knew that if he didn't do something fast, he'd blow like some teenage newbie, rather than the forty-year-old Dom he was. Morgan groaned in frustration and gripped the edge of his desk so he wouldn't come right there, just thinking about Callie and her sexy-as-hell body.

He inhaled slow and deep, then exhaled slowly, trying to push thoughts of Callie and her submissive qualities out of his mind. It wasn't as if anything could happen. Not only did he know she wasn't the right person for him, but he'd made sure she'd never have him. He'd been a complete asshole to her the day before and he knew it. It had been all about self-preservation. If he hadn't tried to push her away while acting like she was nothing but a mere presence in his life, he'd have done something stupid like throw her over his shoulder and carry her back to his house.

Callie Masters was officially turning him into a fucking caveman. All he needed was a club in one hand while he dragged her around by a fistful of hair in the other.

Nope. He needed to stop thinking about fisting anything.

He'd never reacted so quickly, or with such intensity to another person like that before. He'd been almost unable to control himself; as a man who valued control above all else, that scared the shit out of him. Morgan needed to put up boundaries immediately to protect them both.

Now, because Austin put him in this position, he'd have to face the torture of Callie's hands on his body for hours at a time until his tattoo was complete.

And they hadn't even begun the process beyond tracing his back.

He still didn't know why Austin had done that, unless he truly believed Callie would be the perfect person to lay his ink. He'd called the man later and tried to find a polite way to back out of it, but it had been to no avail. Austin believed in his former apprentice and would be right there the whole time, along with his crew, if Callie needed anything. Austin had a way of finding the right tattoo artist for the client, that much Morgan knew, so he couldn't hold back. He would have to trust his friend.

If Morgan had been a more cynical man, he'd have thought his friend wanted to set he and Callie up. That wasn't the way Austin worked though, so Morgan knew it was all in his head. He would deal with Callie and get the ink he desired; that didn't mean it would be easy though. And it sure as hell hadn't been when he sat so close to Callie, inhaling her sweetness and feeling the heat of her body as she traced his back with small, sure and steady hands.

He'd needed to get out of the shop quickly so he could breathe, or he'd have stayed and let her strip him. Let her run her hands over his back while she learned every contour, dip, curve and slope of muscle. The ink he wanted would take more than one session. In fact, he was sure that it could take at least three or four sessions since he wanted it all in color—multiple colors at that.

He wanted a phoenix that rested its head on his shoulder while its body and tail feathers draped down his back and to his hips. Its wings he wanted spread out over his sides and then his arms. That way they were almost full sleeves that could be easily hidden under a suit.

He was past the age of having to prove himself in business. He had held off getting any tattoos that could be deemed in any way unworthy of his family name other than the outline of a starburst on his lower hip. That had been an eighteen-year-old's experiment with a desire that he'd since forced himself to suppress. He'd always loved tattoos. Loved the way they looked on either gender, the way they made the wearer's skin look like a painting on a silk canvas, rather than the degenerates his society made them out to be. He'd been jealous of Austin's talent and the way he wore his art and life on his body. Tattooing was Austin's livelihood, his life; it only made sense that the man could wear whatever ink he wanted— where he wanted.

Morgan hadn't been that lucky. He'd been forced to hide what he wanted and live a life dictated by others—in more ways than one come to think of it—because he couldn't risk offending the board, his family, and those who watched him because of his father and his father's father.

Morgan McAllister was the last male heir of the blue-blooded, old-moneyed McAllisters. And the burden of that legacy along with its responsibilities and expectations weighed heavy on his shoulders. He couldn't do anything to risk disenchanting his mother and sisters. If he acted as he truly desired in his personal life, he'd only hurt them in the process. As much as the women in his life angered and annoyed him to no end, he wouldn't disrupt their lives. He loved them even if he didn't like them most days.

Getting a tattoo would probably cause his mother to have some sort of nervous breakdown, but he knew it was time to take control of his life. He'd long since known he was something of a disappointment to them. He never could conform to their wishes and do exactly what they expected of him.

He'd made sure any unusual...activities he enjoyed were conducted behind locked doors. No one had ever heard so much as a whisper of his name within a club or leather store. No one knew he'd not only been with women, but men as well, though he'd always preferred the former when it came to relationships outside the scene. No one knew he was a Dominant in the bedroom as well as in the boardroom.

He'd waited until his career was no longer under his late father's shadow to become his own person in truth. His dominant personality helped to fast track his career so that by the time he hit thirty, it was no longer a question of how his father would have done it, but now about what Morgan wanted. When he'd turned forty, he decided it was time to make his personal life his own. And he would do his best to ensure that his life did not have a negative impact on his mother and sisters.

So he'd get his tattoo that he could easily cover up. And he would enjoy the pain since he was the one who usually dispensed such sweet ecstasy.

That thought brought with it the image of Callie on her knees and the memory of the spark in her eyes. Hmm. Maybe she wasn't quite so innocent. He'd felt the submissive in her, so maybe that part wasn't quite so suppressed and hidden. Maybe he wouldn't have to tempt her too far and she'd come willingly into his arms and into his bed. The thought of Callie in restraints and a blindfold caused warmth to pool at the base of his cock.

No.

Damn it. He needed to stop thinking like this.

Jesus, he didn't know what was wrong with him. Usually it didn't take so much effort to forget about a woman. Yeah, that sounded like an asshole thing to say, but none of the women he'd been with had thought about him more than what he could do for them. Whether it was his bank account, the women his mother wanted him to be with or the dominance he wielded over the women in his nightlife, none of them were ever allowed to know the real Morgan.

He'd done that on purpose, but now he'd reached a point where he'd never felt lonelier; maybe it was time to find someone who cared about *him*. Someone he could actually grow older with. At forty, the idea of raising babies and chasing children in the yard might not be as easy as it could have been when he was younger, but he could be happy.

Couldn't he?

Callie's face came to mind again and he cursed. She wasn't right for him. This also wasn't about where she'd fit in within his society. He didn't give a flying fuck if the person he fell for had a closet full cocktail dresses and ball gowns. He didn't care if they went to galas and knew about the lives of society's inner circles. He didn't want the perfect society wife. His mother might spend most of her days pushing that exact woman on him, but that didn't mean he would accept her.

Callie was wrong for him because of her age. She was not only too young for him, but she probably hadn't lived as much as he had in her few short years. He didn't want to tarnish an innocent with the dark needs that lived inside him.

He would continue to hold her at arm's length and keep her out of his thoughts.

Sure, like that was working for him, but he would keep trying.

"Morgan? You got time for a quick chat?" Sam, his friend and co-worker said as he walked into Morgan's office.

Morgan nodded and released his grip on the desk. Thoughts of Callie were messing with his job and he would put an end to that in one swift move.

"What can I do for you, Sam?" He had always liked Sam. Morgan wasn't close to a lot of people, including Sam and Austin, but he felt comfortable around the other man. Sam didn't know about Morgan's personal life beyond the glitter and the family responsibilities Morgan let the world see, but that was okay. Only Austin, his friend Decker, and a few others knew what Morgan really did behind closed doors. And that was because they, too, had secrets of their own.

"Are you going to the gala this weekend?" Sam asked as he sat down across from Morgan. The two chairs in front of the desk were slightly lower than Morgan's own and he held back a smile. Call it petty, but Morgan liked the subtle way that gave him leverage. Whoever sat in those chairs would always be at a lower level than Morgan, giving him the slight psychological edge. He might not ever need it, but it never hurt to show the others they would never be on an even playing field.

He was damn good at his job and he would make sure everyone knew it.

Sam's words drifted to him and he frowned. "Gala?" He mentally flipped through his schedule and knew for a fact he didn't have a date then. No, he had his third consult with Callie and her gentle hands actually.

He held back a groan. Best not to think about those hands anywhere on his body when he was at work. Or at home. Or ever.

Fuck. He wasn't sure what he was going to do tonight either considering he had his *second* consult with her so she could show him sketches and get a feel for his back. He wanted to actually start the tattoo the night of the gala. His cock hardened at the thought of her. Shit. He wasn't going to last long at this rate.

Sam rolled his eyes. "Figured you'd get out of it. It's the Clemhouse Foundation's annual art gala. This time I think the proceeds go to inner city art programs or something like that. You went last year; I know since I was there too."

Morgan nodded. He remembered the previous year. He hated events like that. Rich people got dressed up in silks and diamonds and paraded around, showing one another up all in the pretense of helping the less fortunate. He much preferred to donate directly to the cause and even roll up his sleeves and help out, even though his mother felt working with one's hands was beneath their social class. He'd helped build homes, cleaned up parks, and did other manual labor.

Going to a gala so people could stare at him and wonder when he'd finally take a wife and create an heir for his vast fortune wasn't on his top list of things to do.

"No, I'm not going this year." He'd donated directly to the foundation's projects already. That way he knew where the money went without having to deal with people. "I have an appointment anyway."

"An appointment?" Sam asked. His brow rose. "What kind of appointment would you have on a Friday night? Got a hot date?"

Yes, but not exactly how I want it.

Morgan gave Sam a bland look. "Not a date, but I'm not doing the gala either." He could have rescheduled with Callie since it was tentative anyway. They'd put it down on the calendar just in case they were ready after tonight's meeting. If he really needed to go to the gala, he would have; he just didn't want to.

He wanted Callie.

"Wish you were," Sam mumbled. "I hate going to those things without you there. Sally gets a bit crazy with all the preparations and then I have to act like I'm interested." Sally was Sam's 'plastic and perfect' wife. Like most of the people in Morgan's realm, they had been brought together within the proper circles and married young. Morgan figured Sam had loved Sally at one time, but not any longer.

Sam's wandering eye had gotten him in trouble with married women, and Morgan had put a distance between himself and his friend. Sally didn't care about the affairs though, because she had a slew of young men in her sheets...and between her legs. They were the typical moneyed couple. They married because it was expected, had children to continue the dynasty, and sent those children to boarding school to be raised to carry on the proper traditions and produce future heirs. Sam and Sally didn't love each other beyond a few good memories in their youth and spent most of their time staying out of each other's way.

Sally had even approached Morgan a time or two, her blatant flirting sickening him. He'd never told Sam about the time Sally had grabbed his cock through his pants and purred in his ear about how she desired a lover to make her feel like the naughty young girl she was.

Morgan closed his eyes, swallowing back the bile. Maybe it was time to make some new friends.

"You're so lucky you're not married," Sam said, bringing Morgan out of his thoughts. Well, if being married meant treating the other person like an unwelcome relative then cheating on them every time one had a chance, then no, Morgan did *not* want to be married.

"To each their own," Morgan responded. He let out a sigh and ran his hand over his face.

"Was there something you wanted beyond knowing if I was going to the gala?"

"No," Sam answered. "That was pretty much it. Sally and I will be there of course, so if you change your mind, you'll see familiar faces."

He nodded. Although he didn't agree with the way Sam lived, he and Sally never hurt each other behaving as they did. They'd gone into their relationship knowing what the future held. At least that's what Sam told him one drunken night over a bottle of cognac. Morgan couldn't judge what he didn't understand, but that didn't mean he had to live it with them.

"Thanks for letting me know. I don't plan on going, but if something happens, then I'll see you there."

Sam nodded and they talked about business for a few more minutes before he left Morgan to his own devices. He still had to do a few things around the office before he could head to Montgomery Ink to see Callie.

Damn. Maybe he should rephrase that as going to his consult. Less likely for him to imagine fucking her over the bench that way.

Sort of.

"Morgan. There you are."

Morgan closed his eyes and sat very still. Maybe, if he didn't move, she wouldn't see him. He remembered the only time his mother managed to drag him to a movie premiere—*The Devil Wears Prada*. It struck him as more than coincidence that the character Miranda Priestly could have been his mother incarnate.

"Why on earth are you chuckling with your eyes closed? You're at work, for God's sake. Act like your father and not some heathen."

He sighed, then looked up. "Hello, Mother. To what do I owe this visit?"

She narrowed her eyes, her perfectly sculpted eyebrows not moving an inch thanks to the previous week's Botox party. A Botox party for Christ's sake. What would his mother think of next in the never-ending battle against the effects of aging?

"I would have called, but your secretary never puts me through. I'm your Mother; he should show some respect."

Morgan leaned back in his chair, lacing his fingers together over his chest. "Timothy is my administrative assistant, not my secretary. And when you call, you shout at him to give the phone to your son, no matter what meeting I'm in. I do call back when I can, Mother, but this is a business, as you never cease to remind me."

"Your *father's* business," she snapped.

He ignored the ache at his temples just like he ignored the one across his heart at her words. He'd never be good enough for her, never be his father, but he'd long since given up trying.

"It's mine now, Mother. It would do you well to remember that. Now, tell me why you're here," he added before she could snap at him again.

"I'm here to tell you about Heather, your date."

Ah, another woman who was suitable for Morgan according to the McAllister standards, and handpicked by his mother.

Another woman Morgan wanted no part of.

Callie's face flashed in his mind yet again and he forced himself to push it away. He was stronger than this damn it. He wouldn't think about her again.

"No."

His mother waved her hand in the air in a dismissive gesture. "Oh stop being so difficult. Heather is a nice woman. She's a McKinley, their youngest in fact. The others were already snapped up but she's now ready for society and the pressures of being a society wife. She's trained in her duties and will be fine with your wandering eye if that's what it comes to. She's not in it for love, but for your name. If you want to have a few daisies on the side, then keep it quiet. Your father always did. You're not getting any younger and I need grandchildren."

Morgan ground his teeth. There were so many things wrong with what his mother had just said, he didn't know where to start. This wasn't the first woman she'd paraded around him. No, Heather was the latest in an endless line of perfectly sculpted women with even more perfect backgrounds. He wanted no part of that life. His sisters lived it. His mother had. He would not hurt the woman he married. He wouldn't be the man his father had been. While his mother never acted hurt over his father's affairs, Morgan knew better.

"You have grandchildren, Mother." There. He'd start with the easiest part.

"Your sisters have children and I play the doting grandmother."

Playing a doting grandmother? Yes, and she deserved an Oscar for her performance.

"You need an heir, Morgan. Our family legacy cannot and will not end with you."

They'd had this argument countless times before. "My sisters' children will be well provided for no matter what children I bring into the world. We aren't in the ducal system in England. Stop trying to put your pressures on me."

His mother scowled. "You'll never amount to what he wanted for you."

He nodded. "True, because I never wanted to."

She sighed and closed her eyes. "Just go to the gala, Morgan. Take Heather with you. It needs to be done for the family. I don't ask much of you."

"You ask everything of me," he countered, then the guilt that came with his family started to creep in. "What is so important about going on Friday with Heather?"

His mother's eyes flashed in triumph.

Shit.

"She's part of a family we are friends with. It would be good to quell the rumors about your lack of wife to at least be seen with her. You won't have to marry her, just one night of being seen together should work."

He'd heard the rumors but they were so far from the truth, he didn't care. They thought he was impotent or just didn't care for marriage at all. There were no rumors about what he liked in his submissives or what he looked for in a woman or a man for that matter.

Callie came to mind again and he sighed. If he thought about her one more time, he'd agree to go with Heather. He needed to scrub thoughts of the woman he could never have from his mind. Going out with a woman he wanted nothing to do with would help.

He only had to stop thinking about Callie and then he'd not have to deal with either of them.

Doable.

Maybe.

CHAPTER THREE

Callie was going to come. Or at least she hoped she would because this aching feeling wouldn't go away. She arched her back, pushing her head into the pillow so she'd get a better angle. She was in that happy-warm post-nap state and didn't want to fully wake up—not when she had visions of the sexy Morgan McAllister on her brain.

She imagined his hands on her hips, slowly running down her sides and then back up. His hands would be large, warm, and calloused, not smooth and silky. Morgan lowered his head, kissing down her chest in the valley between her breasts, teasing her.

She loved to be teased—not that she'd tell Morgan that. He'd have to find that out all on his own. Morgan licked down her body, laving her belly button before going over the soft roundness of her stomach. She'd never been too skinny and had the curves of a woman who loved her body. The Morgan of her dreams cherished it, told her he loved each and every inch of her. His dream self sucked the hood of her clit; she pressed the palm of her hand on her clit, trying to mimic the pressure he'd give her. He had a sexy mouth and she had a feeling he'd know exactly what to do with it when he was going down on her. He'd show her how talented he was with each lick, each nibble, each suck.

She ran two fingers around her entrance, then slowly inserted them, her body slick and ready. She was already on the edge just by dreaming of him and with only a few touches, she'd come.

Empty and wanting, but she'd come.

She fucked herself with her own fingers while grinding the heel of her hand on her clit. All the while, she imagined the touches as Morgan and not herself. She could have used one of her vibrators but she didn't want to feel anything but skin, not when she was imagining Morgan that afternoon.

Cursing herself when she couldn't quite reach that spot within herself, she increased the pace, dreaming of Morgan fucking her hard with those large fingers of his. She could imagine the rasp of his stubble on the inside of her thighs and on her freshly shaved pussy. That thought sent a delicious shiver down her back as she pushed over the edge. Her feet slammed on the bed, her toes curling into her sheets. She gasped his name as her channel clamped around her fingers. Her orgasm rocked her fast then drifted slowly, leaving a blush and sheen of sweat on her skin.

She lay lax on the bed, one hand in her panties and the other up her shirt cupping her breast. Her breathing finally came down to normal and she relaxed into the bed.

Well that was one way to wake up from an afternoon nap.

It probably would have been better if Morgan had actually been there and it wasn't just her hand, but that would never happen. She slowly removed her hands from her body and sighed when she turned to look at the clock. Well crud. She had to wake up fully now and take a shower if she was going to make it back to the shop.

With a sigh, she rolled out of bed, stumbling to the bathroom so she could wash the scent of her orgasm off her body. There was no way she'd walk into the shop—let alone work with Morgan—when she smelled of her own arousal. Not the best way to remain professional. What the hell was she saying? She's just gotten her rocks off by thinking of the man. There was no way she'd be able to look him in the eye and not remember her dream. Not remember the way his lips sucked on her clit and her pussy.

He had a great mouth, she thought again.

Too bad that mouth would never be on her.

His loss.

She turned on the water, hoping it would at least get to medium hot today. The old water heater for the building was on its way out so she never knew what she'd get. Since it was the afternoon and not early morning with people getting ready for their day, she had a better chance of taking a shower that wouldn't make her nipples more erect than they already were.

She stripped then got in the shower, smiling as the heated water touched her skin. Lucky break. She wouldn't freeze to death before she headed into work. She lathered up, washing her hair quickly and rising off before scrubbing away the scent of her dream. It wasn't unusual for her to take afternoon naps since she was of the mindset that if she was tired and had time, sleeping was always an option, but today had been more about exhaustion than anything else.

Instead of sleeping the night before, she'd been up working on Morgan's sketch. Not only was this going to be a big job—the biggest she'd ever been part of—but it was her first large job on her own. The small tattoos she'd done at the shop in her new station totally counted when it came to her being an artist in her own right, but they had been easy. Morgan was different.

And that was the problem in more ways than one.

Not only did she want to make sure she got it right for herself, but she had the pressure of Austin and Morgan as well. For that matter, the rest of the shop would be looking in on her during the whole process. She didn't fault them for that since the support usually calmed her, but right then, it was a little nerve-wracking.

She wanted it to be perfect. Sure, Morgan had been an asshole to her even though her body and dreams didn't seem to care, but that didn't make it any less true. The need to prove herself to him and everyone else—including herself—drove her.

She wanted him to be proud of the work she'd done and know that she cared about it and she'd put her heart into it. It was a pipe dream. That didn't make it any less true in her mind. She wouldn't be able to stop herself from wanting to please him. There was just something about the way he made her feel, even when he pissed her off.

She didn't even know him and yet something inside her had clicked when she saw him. It wasn't like love at first sight or anything. God, no. It might have been lust at first sight, but it was more of a *need* at first sight.

A need to please and to serve, and the need to find herself within that desire.

In truth, it confused her, so she tried to push that all away and concentrate on his sketches. Since she'd only traced his body she'd done preliminaries that would need to be changed once she felt the dips and curves of his muscles.

In a professional manner, of course.

It wasn't like she was going to feel him up just to get her rocks off.

She snorted. She had her dreams for that apparently.

Since she'd been up the entire night before working on four different sketches, she was a wreck that morning. Luckily she'd only been at the shop to do admin work rather than tattooing. Montgomery Ink didn't have a receptionist right now; they went through them rather quickly, so it fell to all of them to handle the admin work occasionally. Everyone hated it, but if it helped her family, then she was glad to help.

She'd been exhausted, and thankfully, Austin had let her go home for a four-hour nap. Well, maybe *let* wasn't exactly right. More like he put her in his truck, drove her home, set her on her doorstep, and told her to get some sleep. His friend, Decker, had followed them in her car so she'd be able to get back to the shop that evening to meet with Morgan. She smiled at the thought of big, bad Austin worrying about her like he was one of her sisters. Since he was the eldest of eight children—three of them girls—he had a lot of practice telling people what to do. While his brothers and sisters might get annoyed, she kind of liked it. She never had a big brother watching out for her, and now she had Austin, Sloane, and the rest of them.

Not too shabby.

Taking another look at the clock she sighed. She still had time before Morgan would be off work and headed to the shop, so she could either hang out at home and try not to think about him or go to work and do the same. While she might be safer at home with her thoughts so others wouldn't pick up on them, she figured going in and getting coffee while seeing what her family was up to would be a better use of her time.

She grabbed her sketchbooks and her purse, then made her way to her car. She lived close to downtown Denver where the shop was located. Some days she took the bus, but since she was working late, Austin didn't want her on the bus at night. It wasn't that it was an issue of her safety per se; it was more about being careful.

After she arrived at the shop and parked in the back lot, she stopped by Taboo instead of heading right into work. She could not only use the caffeine since four hours wasn't the greatest amount of sleep, but she wanted to see Hailey. She hadn't told her friend about her fascination with Morgan, and she wasn't sure she was going to. It wouldn't do for Austin to find out she had a crush on a man she was inking—a man who looked down on her. Damn, why did she find Morgan worthy of her dreams and orgasms? Just because he was sexy as hell and made her want to kneel for him didn't mean he was good for her. Probably just the opposite.

"Callie, darling, you look like you need coffee."

Callie rolled her eyes at Hailey's words then plunked down next to Miranda, Austin's youngest sister, at the breakfast bar. "Coffee sounds wonderful but if I look like I need it, maybe I should have spent a little more time with my concealer."

Miranda took Callie's chin in hand and studied her face before letting her go. "You look beautiful as always. Your eyes look tired, but only because we know you, not because you have dark circles or anything. I wish I could do fun things with my hair like you, but I don't think that would pass at the job."

Considering Miranda was an elementary school teacher, she was right about that. Miranda even needed to make sure each tattoo her brother or sister inked on her skin was in the safest place possible to avoid offending the parents or the school board.

Callie took a few of Miranda's soft brown strands in her fingers. "Maybe you can do purple tips or highlights in the summer or something."

Miranda snorted. "Uh no. Not unless I left town to do it. They'd know." The younger woman lowered her head, but kept her eyes on Callie making her look devious. "They *always* know."

"You're so cute," Hailey teased as she set coffee and a pastry in front of Callie. "Eat this and then I'll get you real food. The sugar will help for a bit."

Callie nodded then took a bit of the fluffy pastry. "Yum."

"Yum is right. She's amazing." Miranda took a bite of her own pastry. "Oh, and stop calling me cute. I'm only two years younger than you both. It's not like you're Austin or the rest of the other Montgomery's ages."

Callie rolled her eyes and took a sip of her latte. Hailey was a goddess. "Two years is two years and I'll take anything I can get."

"At this point, unless one of my brothers marries someone younger than me, I think I'm screwed in the age department," Miranda said with a fake sigh.

"You like being the baby, so shut up," Callie said without heat.

"Maybe when I was younger, but now? Now it's kind of hard to...well. Never mind." Miranda blushed and Callie raised a brow at Hailey.

"Look at that blush," Hailey said with a smile. "Tell us his name."

Miranda's eyes widened and she shook her head. "Nope. Not going to spill—no matter what baked goods you ply me with." She sat up straighter, then grinned. "How about you tell me about your love lives instead. I can live vicariously though the both of you."

Hailey froze for a moment, the put on a bright smile. "You know I don't kiss and tell."

If there had been any kissing in Hailey's life recently, Callie would eat her shoe; from the look on Miranda's face, she didn't believe it either.

"Fine. Keep your secrets." Miranda turned to Callie. "What about you? Anything we need to know?"

Callie could feel her cheeks warm and she lowered her gaze. She'd come in here to talk to Hailey about Morgan, even if it was just in passing, but now that she had the opportunity, she wasn't sure if she could. She didn't have anything to say anyway. He was just a client. A client who didn't even *like* her.

There was nothing between her and Morgan.

So why couldn't she stop blushing?

Why couldn't she stop dreaming about him while touching herself so she could feel how wet he got her?

"Callie, honey, there's no one in the cafe to hear you," Hailey whispered. "The customers that are eating are way back in the corner and not listening to us since they're involved in their own conversations. You can talk to me and Miranda, you know. It's okay. We're not going to judge."

Miranda leaned closer. "It's not Austin is it?" she said softly and Callie sputtered.

"He's *engaged*, Miranda."

Austin's sister nodded. "I know; that's why I was making sure."

"No, it's not Austin. It's not a Montgomery—as much as it would be cool to be part of your family for real."

Miranda let out a breath and leaned back. "I have other brothers who are single. Plus Maya is single too—if you felt that way."

Callie snorted. "Uh, no, but thanks for auctioning off your family."

"Is it Sloane?" Miranda asked.

Hailey dropped a coffee cup, the shattered remains in pieces around her feet. She blinked up at them, her face pale. "Slippery hands," she mumbled, wiping her completely dry hands on her apron.

Callie stood up to help, but Hailey waved her off. "I've got it, the broom is right here." Miranda met Callie's gaze and Callie shook her head. This wasn't the time or place, and frankly, it wasn't Callie's business.

"It's not Sloane," Callie whispered and Hailey's shoulders relaxed. The woman might not say a thing about her attraction to her friend, but her body language said it all.

"So, who is it then?" Miranda asked, her voice bright. They were all trying to blow past Hailey's reaction and hopefully do a better job of it than they were doing now.

"He's a client," Callie answered then told them about meeting Morgan and what she was doing for him. She left out the rest of the details since her friends didn't need to know those anyway.

"He sounds like a jerk," Miranda said, stirring her drink absently. "A yummy jerk, but a jerk."

"Maybe he had a reason to act that way." Hailey held up her hand. "I'm not condoning his words, nor am I saying dismissing you as nothing more than a pretty girl was right, but maybe there was something else going on."

Callie gave her a wry smile. "It doesn't matter. That something made him push me away and dismiss me. Fine. Whatever. I just need to get over this attraction so I can actually work."

Miranda nodded. "Maybe you should ask him out."

Callie choked on the sip she'd taken. Hailey handed her a napkin, helping her clean up. "Uh, honey, he doesn't want me. I don't need to be dating clients."

The younger woman rolled her eyes. "Oh shut up. You don't know what he wants if he was acting so weird. You can date a client as long as it doesn't screw up your work. I know you won't let that happen. I'm not saying screw him right on the bench, but if you get the attraction out of the way, get the awkwardness of you not knowing what to do out of the way, you can move on. If you feel like there's an opening when you're with him, ask him out. If you don't feel that way, if you don't get that spark, then move on." She met Callie's gaze. "Don't let fear rule you. Don't let the fact you don't know how he feels push you away. Take a chance if you want to. Don't let him get away if you feel something." She let out a breath. "Believe me, watching on the sidelines sucks and I don't want you to be that person."

"I don't either," Hailey murmured.

Callie sighed. She knew Hailey's issues and had a feeling about Miranda's but wouldn't voice it. It seemed all three of them were on the sidelines, not actively working toward what they wanted. The problem was, Callie wasn't entirely sure what she wanted in the first place.

She shook her head and stood up, leaving money for Hailey on the counter. The other woman always tried to force her not to pay, but

Callie would have none of that. Friends paid so bills got paid.

"I don't know what I'm going to do other than give him a kickass tattoo. Whatever happens, I'll deal. I'm sure it's all in my mind anyway."

"Just be yourself and see what happens," Miranda said with a smile.

Callie smiled back, feeling like she could actually make it through a session without freaking. Her friends might have made her think a bit harder about what she was going to do, but she at least had more directions to go rather than into the dark hole of doubt.

She said her goodbyes and walked through the side entrance into Montgomery Ink. Maya was working on someone's sleeve while her friend, Jake, watched. He must have been there to pick her up since he didn't normally watch her work unless they had plans for the evening.

Austin had headed out to be with Sierra and his son, Leif. He'd mentioned his plans to her when he dropped her off at her house. The fact that Austin was a daddy never failed to make her smile. The gruff man had been alone for far too long and now he had a family. Good for him.

She headed to the office to set her stuff down and found Sloane there, painstakingly working on a sketch.

"Hi, Sloane," She didn't want to interrupt, but she didn't want to startle him, either.

"Hey, Callie. You working on that big project for Morgan tonight?"

She nodded, but he couldn't see her since his attention was on his work. "Yep. He should be in soon so I'm going to work on my sketches for him for a few minutes." She bit her lip. "Can I see what you're working on?" Sloane was usually pretty cool with her looking at what he was drawing at all stages of production, but this one seemed a bit different.

It was the hawk for the military vet and she knew he had to be feeling this one a bit more. She didn't know much about his past other than he'd been in the military as well.

He met her gaze, the shadows making her want to hug him.

"Yeah, take a look. I'm almost done."

She nodded and took a look, sucking in a breath. It was beautiful. The hawk spread its wings looking as if it was actually reaching high up into the sky. Each feather looked like it could come off the page if she touched them. Its eye stared at her, and she knew that anywhere she moved, it would look as if it were looking just at her.

"It's beautiful."

She didn't notice she was crying until she tasted salt on her tongue. Undone, she went to her toes and kissed Sloane on the cheek. "You've done a wonderful job. He'll be proud to wear it on his skin."

Sloane stood and took a step back, his jaw clenched.

"You're a good man, Sloane."

He stared at her a moment, then shook his head, and left the room with his sketch in hand.

She cursed. She couldn't heal all of the wounds, but she usually did a better job than picking at them. With a sigh, she quickly dried her face, then picked up her sketchpad and made her way to her station. Sloane was at his own station, but didn't look up. She'd have apologized, but there was nothing to apologize for—not that he would want to hear anyway.

She sat at her station, her attention on the four sketches she'd made for Morgan. He'd been detailed in what he'd wanted, but there was still so much room for interpretation. The idea that it would be one continuous piece over his arms and back going down toward his hips made it hard to ensure he got exactly what he wanted.

She felt him before she heard him.

Her body clenched, her cheeks going warm as he stepped into her station. He didn't make a sound, didn't say a word, but she knew he was there, his gaze on her.

She took a deep breath and turned to him. "Mr. McAllister." She couldn't quite call him Morgan to his face, not when she'd said his name when she'd come on her fingers.

"You can call me Morgan, Callie," he said, his voice a soft growl. "After all, you're about to have your hands on me."

Was he teasing? Flirting with her? Damn it she just didn't know.

"True...Morgan." She stood up, surprised to find her legs were steady. "Why don't you take off your shirt?"

He raised a brow but she didn't falter. Instead she raised a brow of her own.

"I need to see your back to make sure what I have will work." She already knew it would, she'd sketched and traced him fully, but she needed to double check.

"Can I see what you have first?"

"After I see your back."

He didn't move, didn't blink. He didn't seem like a man who heard no too often. Too bad. But he must have found something he liked, because he slowly undid his tie, then unbuttoned his shirt.

She would not drool.

He didn't have an ounce of fat on him. Austin had said Morgan was forty years old, but he didn't look it. Nor did he have the body of a twenty-year-old man. Callie didn't want that anyway. His body had aged beautifully and was clearly well cared for. He had some hair on his chest, but not much. The hair on his belly trailed down to beneath his dress pants and Callie did her best not to swallow her tongue.

She persevered.

Barely.

"Please turn around so I can see the sketches against your back." He did so without comment and she sucked in a breath.

Perfect.

Not even a scar, although scars could be sexy as hell too. Every single sketch of hers would work. She'd traced his body with her pencil and her hands, memorized every inch of him even though she hadn't meant to. His arms would have to be shaved so she could tattoo him, but other than that, he was perfect.

No, not perfect. There was no such thing as perfection and it would do Callie well to remember that.

She cleared her throat. "You can turn around now. I'll show you what I have and we can either start the outline tonight or give you more time to think about it."

He turned and stared at her. "Okay then."

She thought of Miranda's words, thought of what she wanted. It would be a mistake to ask him, yet an even greater one to hold herself back.

"When we're done, we can grab some food if you'd like," she whispered. She hadn't meant to whisper, but saying it any louder was too difficult. The way she put it gave her an out in case he said no. It could have been a dinner with friends and her watching over him to make sure he refueled. Could have been.

Something she read as need washed over his gaze and she held her breath.

"I don't think that would be appropriate," he said softly and she smiled brightly, her heart aching.

Damn it. She shouldn't have put herself out there. But if she hadn't done it, she would never have known for sure. Holding herself back would only have led to worries of what might have been.

Whether he meant appropriate in terms of her being his tattoo artist, her age, or just who they were in respect to one another, she didn't know. Maybe she didn't want to know.

"No problem," she said smoothly. "Just make sure you eat something when you get home. I don't want you to crash on me."

He nodded and then sat down on the stool. "Show me your sketches. If we find one that calls to me, then we can start tonight."

She smiled again, then turned around to pick up her work and compose herself. The blade in her heart from him saying no shouldn't have hurt so much. It wasn't as if she ever stood a chance anyway; they were too different.

She turned around again and showed him her work. This time the nervousness in her belly made her shake a bit. For some reason, this meant more to her than just asking him out for dinner. This was her heart and soul on paper. If he didn't like any of them, she knew she'd have to turn him over to Austin. She'd put everything she had into what Morgan held in his hands and she knew she didn't have the heart to do it again.

Morgan didn't say anything, his attention on her work. She tried not to bounce from foot to foot, but failed.

"Each of them follows the same premise," she explained. "The colors can be changed, but I do think the pallet for each of them works well. I like the phoenix over your left shoulder, rather than your right and the tail leaning more toward the right hip; that way, it's not too symmetric, but not too one-sided either." She forced herself to shut up. He didn't need to hear her ramblings.

He looked into her eyes and she held her breath. "They are all amazingly detailed and beautiful." He shook his head. "I wasn't expecting such breathtaking work."

She ground her teeth but didn't say anything. For all she knew, he didn't mean her talents, but meant what he would be seeing on paper.

"I enjoyed it," she said honestly.

He looked down at the art in his hands one more time. "I can tell." He handed her one, her favorite, that held blues and purples so rich she'd love to see it blend on his skin. "This one. This one is perfect."

She smiled. "That's my choice as well."

He met her gaze and she wanted to say more, but held herself back. "Let's get started then."

"Yes. Let's." It would kill a bit of her to keep her hands on his body for the next couple of hours, but she'd do it. She was a professional after all and Morgan McAllister was just a client.

And maybe if she said it often enough, she would believe the lie.

CHAPTER FOUR

This had been a mistake. Morgan gave no outward sign of his frustration and agitation. He maintained an outward expression of disinterested courtesy as he watched the other guests mix and mingle. It would do him no good to make clear his disdain for their pompous hypocrisy.

He was above that.

Barely.

He had promised himself that if he thought about Callie one more time, he would go to the gala with Heather. And now here he stood. He honestly thought he'd be strong enough to control his will, to control his desires. How little he knew about himself and his attraction to his tattoo artist.

As soon as he'd left the shop, she remained on his mind. Her scent had permeated his skin especially around the partial outline. He could do nothing about the dreams, his thoughts, and his need when it came to her. He had to put an end to this for both their sakes.

Instead of succumbing to what was fast becoming an obsession, he'd called his mother and told her to let Heather know he'd reconsidered. Apparently, that had not been necessary since his mother, conniving and devious as she was, hadn't bothered to tell Heather he'd said no in the first place. This woman who had allowed him to be raised by nannies and boarding school faculties spoke to him with what he knew was a facade of cold courtesy - not exactly unpleasant and not unusual for her.

That was how he now found himself at the gala with Heather on his arm and a headache that wouldn't go away. He couldn't push the thoughts of Callie away any more than he could stop breathing.

Now he was stuck at a function he'd told himself he wouldn't attend with a woman who was completely wrong for him. Heather was fake, her hair color, her rack, her cheekbones, her lips—hell, even the curve of her ass didn't look natural. Morgan had no problem with plastic surgery; it was a fact of life in the society he lived in. What bothered him was that people lied about it when it was obvious they'd had a nip here and a tuck there—even major 'body work'. And then those same people would put others down who chose to age gracefully or were obviously satisfied with how they looked and who they were.

Let's hear it for the rampant insecurities of the very rich and shameless.

How his mother had thought this woman would be good for him, he'd never understand. His mother didn't know him, though, so he couldn't really blame her. She'd never tried to get to know him more than superficially, and he'd long since given up caring.

Heather wasn't speaking to him right then, thankfully. Instead she was talking to one of her acquaintances about dresses, or maybe it was about the women who wore those dresses. He didn't know or care, but he'd satisfied his obligation and made an appearance at this function, so he might as well try to be cordial.

The spot between his shoulder blades started to itch, and he had to take a deep breath so he wouldn't start scratching like some ape. Callie had worked on his back for over three hours. She'd talked during some of that time when he needed her voice to get through the pain. It hurt when she'd gone high on his shoulders and her voice had helped. She'd been gentle, even when she was digging a needle into his skin. Her hands didn't shake at all and was professional. His mind had gone to dirty, sweaty places and he had to force himself to keep his erection at bay. It hadn't worked entirely since he'd had a hard-on during the whole damn process, but he at least looked like he was in control.

He didn't remember getting the silly starburst on his lower belly and hip. It had been a teenage mistake that only few saw unless they were naked with him. He figured it had probably hurt like hell, but he'd been too much of a *man* to let on about it. Last night though, he'd grunted and cursed when Callie had gone over a particularly sensitive area over and over to get the outline just right.

It seemed as soon as he'd gotten used to the needle in his skin for a long line, she'd pick it up and start again. She'd soothed him, though, and that had made him want her more. Not something that pleased him in the slightest considering he'd been trying *not* to think of her. Their session was most likely the first of four. She'd done the big outline on his back and it surprised him that she'd done so much in such a short period of time. When he mentioned that she shook her head, telling him it was easy because he'd been so still. The coloring and his arms would actually take longer, hence the next few sessions. Those sessions would be over weekends and be longer than just over the three hours this one had been.

By the time they were through and she'd taught him about aftercare—telling him about using a spatula to get those hard-to-reach places on his back with the special lotion he needed to use—it was late, and he hadn't wanted to leave. What he wanted to do was ask her to come with him so she could help him with his back, even though that would have been a lame excuse. He didn't and walked her to her car since it was late. He hadn't said a word, just looked into her eyes and turned on his heel so he wouldn't do something stupid like kiss her senseless against her car.

He hated the fact he'd had to leave her and he hated it more that he had to turn her down before they even started. Though she'd phrased her request for dinner as if it was an everyday occurrence and purely professional, they both new it wasn't. He'd desperately wanted to say yes to her and have her sit at his table while he fed her from his hand. He'd wanted to care for her as a Dominant would his submissive and have her care for him as well.

He'd cursed himself for those thoughts even as he'd been polite—or as polite as he could be considering that on the inside he'd been screaming *yes*.

She'd done her best to sound friendly and yet he knew that she wanted to take care of him as well. She wanted to ensure he'd eat afterward and take it easy. While he would have loved to let that happen, he knew he couldn't. He was too old for her, to big. He'd scare her. Despite the fact he sensed strongly that she was a submissive, he had no clue about her experience. He'd never know.

It didn't matter that she didn't move in his circles. He hoped she'd understand that, but in order to tell her that, he'd have to let on that he was interested in her. That wouldn't be happening.

He'd hurt her though. He'd seen it in her eyes and he regretted that.

"Morgan, darling, where is your mind?"

Morgan turned to Heather and tried not to recoil at her touch. He shouldn't have come to the gala and doing his mother's bidding by taking Heather was going to have consequences he should have considered beyond trying to get Callie out of his head. Now he was stuck with a woman he truly had no desire to see again and no desire for whatever deeds his mother hoped would happen at the end of the evening.

"Morgan? Darling?"

I'm not your darling.

"What is it, Heather?" He spoke softly, cool and impersonally courteous. *Why did he allow himself to be manipulated into these situations?*

Damn it all.

"Did you hear what I was saying?"

He looked down into her shrewd, calculating eyes and shook his head. "No, I was thinking about a project at work. What is it?"

She pouted like a small child, her lower lip stuck out. "If you don't find me interesting, maybe I'll go talk with your mother." She stroked his arm as she said it and he had to swallow the bile in his throat.

A manipulative idiot; nice one, Mom.

"No, I'm back now. What is it you were saying?" *Don't go to my mother, you calculating bitch. I don't need to have to deal with her and you too.*

"I was talking about your sisters, but that is done now I suppose. You know about the pregnancy, I take it?"

He nodded though he had no idea who was pregnant. His mother might have told him, but he hadn't listened. It wasn't that he didn't care for his sisters—he did—he could only take them in small doses. He loved his nieces and nephews, and if his sisters actually raised them instead of giving them to nannies and boarding schools, he might have been closer to them.

He tried, he really did, but there was only so much he could do when they were not his children.

He didn't have children and didn't plan on having any since he'd closed himself off from the idea of ever settling down. First, it was because he'd been too busy trying to step out of his father's shadow while learning to run the company at the same time. Then it was because he needed to find out on his own what he wanted, rather than living under his mother's thumb.

He knew what he didn't want, which was more than some people could say, but did he know what he *wanted*?

Callie's face popped into his mind and he shook it away.

She wouldn't be good for him.

He knew that.

He just needed to remind himself of it. Often.

Heather was still talking and he nodded in all the right places. If she'd been saying anything of consequence instead of gossiping about who was sleeping with whom and who was down on their luck because of poor investments, maybe he'd listen. Instead he tried to keep his mind off the woman he shouldn't want while planning a way to get out of the building as soon as he could.

"Anyway, darling, Daddy and Mother are planning a trip to Italy to summer but I'm not sure if that's where I will go. Where will you summer next?"

Who the hell summered anymore?

Where his mother and sisters spent the summer was none of his concern. He had a company to run and a woman to forget. Yes, work would help him forget.

As if he'd drawn her out of thin air, Callie walked into the room and a hush rolled over the crowd like a wave.

She was here.

How could she be here?

He shook his head, trying to clear his thoughts. Why shouldn't she be here? He didn't know her well, although the attraction he felt for her made it feel like he did. For all he knew, this was also her social circle and she was just new to *his* life. She could be moonlighting as a tattoo artist and come from money for all he knew.

Heather was whispering to one of her friends and he had a feeling it was about Callie. In fact, from the way others discreetly—and some not so discreetly—glanced at Callie while they whispered, he knew Heather wasn't the only one who had noticed the new arrival.

He let his gaze rake over her, taking in every detail.

She wore a black dress that draped over her body like it was made for her, but from the fabric he knew it hadn't been. Unlike the others in the room, this one was off-the-rack and not as expensive as what every other lady in this room wore.

It didn't matter.

She made the dress.

It covered one shoulder and left the other bare. Dear God, he wanted to lick every inch of her. It was as if she was teasing him showing just that bit of skin. She didn't wear any jewelry except for small black earrings. The ink she wore like a proud badge was enough adornment to make her look like she was a princess.

A sexy, exotic one at that.

She was out of place and everyone knew it. He saw the others murmur around him and he held back a curse. What did they know? How did they think they were better than her? He'd never once thought that. Money and designer clothes didn't make the woman...or the man.

But Callie was clearly being judged—and found wanting.

Callie's face didn't show any response to the whispers, the looks, the judgments. No, she looked...happy. Proud.

He finally looked to her left to her date and the bottom of his stomach fell out.

No, he had to be wrong. It couldn't be.

He knew the man on Callie's arm.

The *married* man on her arm.

Well, fuck.

He hoped to hell she didn't know Matt was married to another woman—a pretty and sweet woman named Virginia. Because if Callie did know Matt was married? Jesus. She was just like the rest of them, wasn't she? Everyone around him cheated and enjoyed it. It was a game to them. How many people could they screw without the world knowing? It didn't matter that they broke their vows; it was all about some selfish need, some insecurity, and making sure their reputations stayed intact. As long as there were no whispers, it didn't matter what they did.

Discretion was key.

Matt appearing at a gala attended by most of the influential people in Morgan's world with his mistress on his arm was not discreet.

Matt was young. New to their world. New to his company.

He was also an idiot.

An idiot that Callie had chosen.

She'd asked Morgan out, shared the heat between the two of them because there was no way she hadn't been affected. He'd felt it, seen it on her face, and he'd seen the way her nipples hardened whenever he was near.

The fact that he was with Heather that night meant nothing. His appearance with Heather was to pacify his mother; it was also a complete lapse in judgment on his part. One he would never allow to happen again.

And Callie was here on the arm of a married man. Maybe she wasn't as innocent as he thought.

"Look at that trash he brought with him," Heather's friend whispered.

"I know," Heather answered. They were quiet, but with the way their voices rose with the crowd, the majority of whom were clearly discussing Callie, he knew she had to be hearing this. "Look at those tattoos? Where did he pick her up? The street?"

Morgan ground his teeth together. This was one reason he'd held off getting the ink he'd desired. If they only knew where Callie's hands had been the previous night...where he *wanted* her hands that night.

"Dear God, what the hell was Matt thinking?" Sam said as he walked up to Morgan, Sally on his arm.

"I know, I mean look at those tattoos," Sally sneered. "That hair. Who does she think she is?"

"You can't just come into our world looking like some prison reject," Heather added in.

They weren't whispering anymore.

He should have been defending her. He knew it, but he couldn't, not when he thought she was part of the world he'd pushed away. She was one of *them*.

A mistress.

A cheater.

Just another in a long line of people in his life who had broken their promises. Marriage vows meant nothing to these people.

Another reason he'd never been married. What was the use when words meant nothing?

"He and Virginia are still together I take it?" he asked softly. His gaze remained on Callie but she hadn't seen him yet. Instead her focus was on Matt and a painting they seemed to be talking about. She laughed and Morgan clenched his jaw.

Sam raised a brow and Morgan wanted to take his question back. He *never* bothered himself with gossip. The fact he'd asked about Matt and Virginia meant something and Sam caught on right away.

"They're together as far as I know," Sam said slowly. Morgan didn't bother to look at him again. He didn't want to see that knowing gaze. "Matt is an up and coming lawyer in his firm. He'll be partner one day as long as he learns to keep his...proclivities to himself."

Callie looked over at Morgan then, meeting his gaze. Her eyes were bright, but not with happiness.

No, it was obvious she knew what others were saying about her, what she assumed he was saying about her.

She looked over at the people around him, one by one, then back at him.

She stiffened slightly and he wanted to shout that she was wrong.

It would have been a lie though.

She was clearly aware of what the others thought and now he was sure she knew he thought so too.

She gave him a tight smile, then turned back to Matt who led her to another painting.

If he'd wanted to make sure that Callie would never want him, he'd just made that a certainty.

Well, hell.

CHAPTER FIVE

I can't believe people can be so fucking stupid."

Callie nodded at Matt's words, her nails digging into his arm. When he winced, she pulled back, softly patting the grooves she'd left. She needed to control herself better than that.

"Sorry."

Matt cursed again before moving his arm so it was around her waist. He leaned closer so others couldn't hear them and she calmed at her friend's closeness. "Why are you sorry? What on earth did you do? You came with me to a freaking gala. A gala I didn't want to go to in the first place and now people are being idiots. I wish I could have gotten out of it because now I want to bash people's heads together for the way they are treating you. Whispers or not, it's still fucking annoying."

Callie sighed and pulled him closer to one of the paintings. People weren't near them so they wouldn't be able to hear what she said. In fact, the others had left a wide swath between them as if they would catch some kind of cooties if they got too close.

Matt was right.

The people in this room were fucking stupid.

"Don't pay them any mind, Matt," she said softly. She tried to smile as she said it but she was afraid it came out as more of a sneer. Maybe even with a grimace. "We're friends. We've been friends since I let you marry *my* friend Virginia."

He laughed roughly, and Callie relaxed somewhat. She'd tried to make him laugh, and though it hadn't been one of his normal, deep belly laughs, it was at least something. Matt was one of the nicest guys she knew and usually didn't get angry so quickly. The fact that he seemed to want to bash heads together told her exactly how much the others and their petty whispers and glares dug into her friend's psyche. While she might want to go scratch out a few eyes—the blonde on Morgan's arm in particular—she wouldn't succumb to temptation.

In fact, she wouldn't be succumbing to *any* temptation in the near future.

She was done with that. Done with any dreams, heated naps, or allure that could move her to do something she'd regret. She'd been stupid to think that she could have a man who obviously thought he was better than she. There was nothing wrong with her, her life, what she loved or what she did for a living. The fact that he seemed to think she wasn't *appropriate*? Well, fuck him.

"And I will thank you every day until the end of my days for letting me have your friend," Matt said, interrupting her tumultuous thoughts. "That doesn't, however, make me feel any better for putting you in this situation."

She shook her head, annoyed with herself for letting her thoughts go down a path that wasn't good for anyone. "No, you didn't put me in any situation. The people in this room with their little brains and high chins are the ones who did that. I came here because you're my friend and you needed me. Plus I happen to like art. I'm fine, Matt. Stop worrying about me." She wasn't fine, but she wasn't going to tell him that.

If Morgan hadn't been there—and boy, oh boy, hadn't *that* been a surprise—she'd have gotten through the evening without a problem; yet the man who plagued her dreams made an uncomfortable situation even worse. His presence at this...party rocked her self-confidence to its core.

Damn him.

No man should be allowed to make her feel like she wasn't good enough. She'd let him get too close. No, that wasn't it. He hadn't been close to begin with. Instead, she'd let the mere thought of him, the dream of a man who didn't really exist, hurt her. That was on her.

"Callie, honey, you came with me because you're my friend and yet I'm screwing you over."

She pushed Morgan firmly out of her mind and faced Matt. "You didn't screw me over. Your wife is sick, Morgan. Virginia has the freaking flu and couldn't come to this thing with you. She's the one who called me. I'm the one who accepted her proposal. All you've done is get me into a pretty dress and take me out for a night on the town because your wife asked you to. There's no fault in that." He'd even offered to buy her a dress in case she didn't have one. She didn't have a dress that satisfied these people's standards, but she had a dress that looked damn good on her. Matt and Virginia didn't pity her, never patronized her, and would never offend her by offering her charity despite the vast difference in their net worth. Callie thought she would be fine.

Apparently she'd been wrong.

She fingered the side of her dress then paused. She wouldn't feel bad about the polyester/rayon blend she wore compared to the silks, satins, velvet and fancy linen around her. She'd never valued expensive clothes and she wouldn't now. She liked what she had and was happy with it.

Her friend narrowed his eyes at the movement. "There *is* a fault in that when the people who are supposed to be my friends are talking about you behind your back." He paused. "No, it's not behind your back since we can hear them and they're not doing a good job about hiding what they think."

She didn't think the others in the room had been trying to hide and that had been the point.

"These people aren't your friends and you know it," she said softly, trying to take the sting out of her words.

He gave her a wry smile. "True. They're my colleagues and clients. My true friends are the ones who drop everything in their lives to come to something like this so I won't look like a complete idiot about art." He grimaced. "I have no idea what art is, Callie. I like what I like, but I don't know if it's good or not. That's what Virginia does. She leads me around and is the best wife I could have ever asked for. She knows what to do for dinners, galas, and other parties. She does all of that and grades papers every night because she works too hard. I love her so much, Callie, and she isn't here."

She smiled at Matt's words. It was true that he had no idea about art or even how to act in a world he hadn't grown up in. While she and Virginia had always been on the poor side growing up, Matt had been solid middle class. Because of good grades, scholarships, and just being an amazing person, Matt had gone to an Ivy League school and was now an associate lawyer in a prestigious firm. He'd made something of himself and had found Virginia, a schoolteacher with the biggest heart Callie had ever seen, along the way.

They were such a cute couple.

A couple that didn't quite fit into this societal mold, but were just fine.

And now that he'd brought Callie with him, he'd probably taken a step or two back in the eyes of those that thought they were her betters.

They couple would be fine and Matt would recover, but rumors were rumors.

She honestly didn't care what people thought, and on a normal night, Matt wouldn't either. He was just stressed not only over a case, but because he'd been forced to leave his sick wife at home alone. He couldn't miss tonight's event, even if coming with Callie put a stain on his reputation. It probably would have been worse if he hadn't come at all since he was so new in the firm.

Maybe if Callie didn't have the tattoos and funky hair, they could have pulled it off. She just hadn't known what to expect in Matt's new world.

Now she knew.

And she wanted no part of it.

She'd shrugged off the looks, the whispers, and the words that were spoken in not-so-hushed tones at first. It wasn't like she'd ever see these people again, so who cared what they thought of her? Matt, however, would have to deal with the consequences of the others' mistaken judgments, but he'd live through it. He and Virginia were tough.

She would have been fine.

Then she'd seen Morgan.

The look on his face...

Damn, she thought she was tougher than that. It wasn't as if he was hers.

He wasn't.

He'd shot that down quickly.

She apparently wasn't what he wanted. As he put it, she wasn't *appropriate*.

Matt sighed from beside her and she turned to her friend. "What's going on?" she asked, pulling her thoughts from the man who'd hurt her with just one glare.

"I need to call Virginia," he said softly and she grinned.

"Why? Because it's been twenty minutes since you've talked to her?" she teased.

He blushed and her body relaxed. She'd come to this event to help her friends and that's just what she'd do. Screw the others with their small minds and big mouths.

"Shut up, Callie," he murmured and she leaned into him. The whispers around them increased and she had to bite her tongue so she wouldn't turn around and bite back.

"Go call your woman. I'll be okay here. Honest," she added when he gave her a look.

Matt kissed her forehead, his hand tangling in her hair—the same thing he'd done for years—and she wanted to kick him. Seriously? He was going to act like the big brother he felt like in front of all these people? They wouldn't see that as a friendly, non-sexual kiss. Instead they'd see it as flaunting his mistress. In public no less. She wanted to curse and throw something, but that wouldn't solve anything. So, she lifted her chin and studied the painting in front of her. Maybe if she kept her attention on the beautiful strokes, the subject of the painting, she could ignore the others circling around her like sharks that smelled blood in the water.

"And who might you might you be, dear?"

Callie grimaced and turned to see an older woman in a dark dress and pearls. Lots of pearls. She pasted on a smile and tried to play the game. The game she had no possible chance of winning since she didn't know all the rules, but she would go down fighting, damn it.

"Callie Masters." She didn't hold her hand out since this woman didn't seem the type to lower herself to touch those she thought beneath her. Normally, Callie wouldn't judge so quickly, but there was something about this woman that set her teeth on edge. "And you would be...?"

The woman raised a brow, as if she'd expected Callie—and everyone else in the vicinity—to know who she was. Too bad Callie wasn't part of this circle. Thank God.

"I'm Eleanor McAllister."

McAllister? Surely not. This couldn't be Morgan's mother. Maybe his aunt or something. Or maybe McAllister was a common name. There was a general resemblance to Morgan, but those shrewd eyes were identical to Morgan's and Callie knew this woman was a close relative at the very least.

Of all the galas in all the world...

The woman didn't like her; that much was certain. Callie could just imagine what would happen if Eleanor McAllister found out about the dirty, dirty dreams and thoughts Callie had about Morgan. Did women still have fainting spells in societies like this? What was the word? Oh yeah, swoon. Or maybe even have the vapors.

"It's nice to meet you," she lied. This woman wasn't speaking to her to make friends, of that Callie was sure. In fact, this woman was the first person at this shindig to dare speaking to Callie. No good could come of this but Callie wasn't about to make things worse for Matt by acting like a bitch.

Eleanor raised a single brow. "Is it?"

Callie blinked, unsure what to say to that. She *hated* being clueless in any situation.

Eleanor's gaze traveled up and down her body, that dismissing sneer growing sharper with each passing second. Nothing like being dismissed.

"Is there something I can do for you?" Callie was done with trying to be nice. She wouldn't go flat out crazy and tell this woman and her friends who silently stood off in the corner watching this interaction exactly what she felt, but she wouldn't stand by and let others tear her down either. She could walk that fine line, damn it.

Eleanor met her gaze, her eyes full of contempt. "You're not wanted here, girl. You should know your betters and go back to the street corners and gutters you came from."

Callie sucked in a breath. The nerve of this woman. "Matt is my friend. If you spent less time judging others and more time working on your people skills, you wouldn't have so many wrinkles around your mouth." She snapped her mouth shut and cursed herself.

Jesus. Way to go, Callie. Way to fucking go.

"You little slut," she whispered. "You're ruining a man who didn't have much to lose in the first place. If you're going to roll in the hay with him, do it privately. Don't throw it in our faces. I don't care if that young man is your *friend*. Get out of here or I will ruin him. He should know better than to bring his trash here on his arm."

Callie balled her hands into fists and opened her mouth to snap back, but stopped when she saw Morgan come up behind Eleanor.

"Mother" He spoke quietly, his voice deep—and cold as ice. Callie's body betrayed her at the sound of his voice and Eleanor caught it.

Damn, damn, *damn*.

"Morgan, darling. Leave this to me. I need to teach this tramp a lesson. She should have known better than to come here among decent people."

"That's enough," he said firmly. "Go back to your *friends*."—the derision was crystal clear—"and I will deal with this."

Deal with this? What the hell did he mean by that? God, she needed to remember that he didn't like her. He was courteous, even nice every once in awhile, but he didn't want her.

She couldn't forget that—not and keep her heart intact.

"Morgan—"

"Enough." He cut her off and met Callie's gaze. "Come with me."

Her back stiffened at his tone, but Callie knew that she would probably be better off with him than with the growing crowd. Sure he was an asshole who's look told her he thought she was a whore, but she still knew him better than she knew anyone else since Matt wasn't there. This was just great.

"You know this woman, Morgan?" Eleanor asked, her voice dripping poison.

"Who I know and what I do is not your concern. You're making a scene, and God knows you hate those. Go save your precious reputation and stop acting like an old snake."

Callie's eyes widened. She'd thought Morgan's tone with her had been harsh, but the one he'd used with his mother made her want to wince. He certainly seemed to hold no affection for her. Now she was as confused as ever.

Morgan held out his arm and she took it after hesitating for a moment. His eyes narrowed when she did so, but she held her chin up. They walked through the room toward the balcony and she tried to ignore the voices around her, their confusion and interest stabbing at her like a thousand claws.

She'd made a mistake and she knew it.

She never should have come and she damn sure shouldn't have taken Morgan's arm.

"I'm sorry about that," he said as soon as they were alone on the balcony.

The words didn't soothe her like he probably wanted. Instead she kept her back straight, forcing herself not to lash out, or worse, cry. She was stronger than this and she had to remind herself of that.

"Sorry about what? The fact that everyone here thinks I'm Matt's mistress? The fact that they would actually think that Matt would cheat on his wife, my friend Virginia? Or how about when your mother called me a slut? Hmm? No, how about this...how about when you looked at me like you thought all of that was true? You honestly thought I was a whore. Well fuck you, Morgan. I know you don't think I'm good enough for you and the people you call friends, but hell, I thought you were better than that. I thought that you actually got to know me just a little. Enough that you wouldn't automatically jump to the conclusion that I had to be screwing the married man I came with or *any* married man for that matter. Did you even ask me why I was here? No. You just automatically thought I was a slut. Thanks for that."

Her chest heaved and to her horror, she tasted salt on her tongue. She quickly wiped her face, pissed off at herself for breaking down.

Damn it. She'd made a mess of it.

Morgan shocked her by brushing a tear away with his thumb. They both sucked in a breath, their gazes meeting.

81

"I'm sorry," he repeated. "So fucking sorry you had to go through that."

"You're not denying what you thought, though," she whispered. Pain sliced through her but she ignored it. She had to move on and grow up. Making herself feel worse for other's thoughts and actions wouldn't help.

Morgan cursed then took her face in his hands, surprising them both. "Yes. I thought that." She opened her mouth to speak but he stopped her. "I thought that because I'm a bastard and I used my past experiences with the people around me to judge you. The people here..." he let out a breath. "Let's just say the people here don't mind cheating as long as you don't put it out in front of everyone like it looked like you and your friend were doing."

She closed her eyes and pulled away. She missed his touch, but she couldn't think when he held her face like that. "I didn't care when the others thought that." She paused. "Well, I cared a little because I hate judgmental people. It was more that they were hurting Matt, you know? He didn't do anything wrong except bring a friend into the lion's den. Gah! People are nuts. But you know what hurt worse?" She should be holding her tongue with this part, but she'd already asked him out the day prior so she might as well let it all hang out there.

"What hurt worse, honey?"

Honey? She wasn't his honey. "What hurt the most was that you thought that. I...I was just...disappointed." Broken. Rejected. Hurt.

He clenched his jaw and reached out to touch her again, only to stop himself. "I regret that my actions, or lack of them when it came to not defending you in time, hurt you. I should have known you wouldn't have been with Matt that way. Hell, I should have known Matt wouldn't have done that. He loves his wife too much and any fool can see that. I came to save you from my mother because no one deserves her lectures and I heard what you said to her."

She sighed. "So until that moment, you still thought I was Matt's mistress? Is that the word your kind uses? Mistress?"

"Callie..."

"No, don't worry. I know you didn't mean to be an ass, it just comes naturally." She tried to grin as she said it, but she was pretty sure it came out with a bit more bite.

Morgan looked at her with an expression she couldn't read and opened his mouth to say something.

"Morgan, there you are," the blonde that had been on his arm earlier came to his side. Okay, crawled like an alley cat protecting its last meal, but whatever. She wrapped herself around him, her mouth in a pout. "You left me alone in there and I didn't know where you'd gone. You know Daddy doesn't want me left alone."

Callie barely resisted the urge to roll her eyes. Dear Lord. Was this the type of woman Morgan wanted? No wonder he'd blown her off. Christ on a cracker.

Morgan's jaw clenched and Callie held back a smile. He brought this woman, so he'd have to deal with all that entailed. "I left you with your friends, Heather. I didn't realize I needed to put you on a leash as well."

The other woman narrowed her eyes then looked directly at Callie. Instead of withering under her glare, Callie raised her chin.

"I see it should have been me who put *you* on a leash," Heather snapped. "What are you thinking, talking to this...this...whore?"

Callie sucked in a breath. What the hell was wrong with these people? She'd never been called so many names from people she'd never met before. That was saying something considering the neighborhood she'd grown up in.

Morgan growled.

Growled.

Kind of hot.

He turned to Heather, gripping her other arm. "Watch your mouth. Don't you dare call her a whore. Do you understand me?"

Warmth filled Callie's chest at his defense of her. That didn't mean all was forgiven though.

Heather widened her eyes then sputtered. Not an attractive look. "You're defending this...person?" The woman's utter contempt for Callie was crystal clear. "She isn't one of us! She's here with that stupid lawyer when he *should* be with his wife. You know the way of things. You keep your treats behind the scenes.

You don't parade your tramp around for all to see."

Jesus, these people were tiring. Callie didn't understand how they could live the way they did, and honestly, she didn't even want to try to understand. As much as her body wanted Morgan, as much as she thought she'd felt a connection, it wasn't worth it. She rubbed her temple, hoping Matt would be back soon so she could just go home.

"Go away, Heather. This was a mistake."

"What? How *dare* you. I'm going to go tell your mother."

Morgan snorted. "Go ahead. I'm forty fucking years old, woman. Do you really think I care what my *mother* says?"

"You brought me with you, didn't you?"

He risked a glance at Callie that she couldn't interpret. "I only brought you out because I was trying to forget someone. Clearly it didn't work."

Callie blinked. Was he talking about her? She didn't know what to think about that. On one hand, the fact that he'd been thinking about so much made her warm again. However, the fact he'd taken Heather out to forget her, well, that sucked. Maybe she wasn't cut out for this after all.

"Callie, there you are," Matt made his way to their side.

Oh great, now it was one big party.

Matt frowned as he looked at the three of them then held out his hand to Morgan. Never let it be said that Matt wasn't a gracious man.

"Hello. Morgan McAllister right? I'm Matt Loren."

Morgan didn't smile when he shook Matt's hand, but he didn't look upset at the interruption either. "Hello Matt, nice to finally meet you."

Matt looked between the three of them, still frowning. "Am I interrupting something?"

"No," Callie said at the same time as Morgan and Heather said, "Yes."

Matt's eyebrows rose, but he didn't question them. "Okay then." He turned to Callie. "I'm sorry, honey, but we need to cut this night short."

Thank God. Then what he said registered and she gripped his arm. "Is Virginia okay?" God, what was she doing? Was Virginia's flu worse? Matt gave her a small smile. "She's okay. Well, not worse anyway." He looked down at his shoes and laughed softly. "I just miss her. Yeah, I'm a sap. Sue me. I shouldn't have come here, Callie. You know that. I hate the fact she's sick and I can't help her, but not being by her side makes it worse. I'm going to head home and drop you off okay?"

She put her arm around him and hugged him to her side fully aware Heather and Morgan were watching them. "You're a good man, Matt. Don't worry about dropping me off, okay? I'm in the opposite direction from you and it makes no sense for you to take the time when Virginia is waiting for you. I only let you pick me up because Virginia insisted. I'll catch a cab. Go and take care of your wife."

"Are you sure, honey?" he asked, a hopeful look in his eyes.

"Of course, dork. Go to your wife and stop worrying about me. I've got this handled."

"I'll drive her home."

Callie froze at Morgan's words, then looked at him, a brow raised.

"Are you sure?" Matt asked.

Morgan nodded, his gaze on Callie, not Matt. "Go home to your wife. You're a good man for wanting to be with her. I'll take good care of Callie."

A delicious shiver ran up her spine at his words.

Bad, Callie. Bad.

"You're what?" Heather yelled.

Morgan silenced her with a look then turned back to Matt. "Go home. I've got this."

Matt sighed then kissed Callie on the cheek. "Thank you. Call me when you get home. Okay?" He gave her a look that told her he'd want the full story later and she smiled. Yep, she'd have to deal with an inquisition at some point. He leaned down to whisper. "If you want me to get you a cab right now, we can run."

She laughed softly. "I'm fine."

Matt nodded and said his goodbyes before leaving. What Callie wouldn't give to be the recipient of such love and devotion.

"You are *not* taking her home. You are here with me. What will people say?" Was this Heather person actually *pouting*?

Callie closed her eyes. She didn't want to deal with this woman.

"I don't care what people will say, Heather," Morgan answered smoothly. "That, after all, is what you care about. Go to my Mother since she drove you here anyway." Callie's eyebrows crept upward at that. They didn't come together? Interesting. "She's the one who wanted you to come so you can deal with her."

"You're a bastard," Heather spat.

Morgan didn't blink. "Yes. Yes, I am. You should remember that. I'm not so easily played. Now, I'm going to go take Callie home since she's been through enough tonight thanks to us."

Heather glared at Callie, then stomped away, not doubt to tell all of Callie's whorish escapades.

When they were alone, Callie couldn't look at Morgan. She didn't know what to think. So much had happened in such a short time and yet still not enough; she didn't know him at all.

"You don't have to take me home, you know. I can just take a cab. I know you were just doing a favor for Matt."

"No, I was more concerned about you. And I *will* be taking you home."

"You can't tell me what to do," she said when she looked at him.

He gripped her chin, hard. "Can't I?"

She opened her mouth but couldn't speak.

88

That's what she was afraid of. She wanted him to order her, wanted him to tell her what to do, how to please him.

If she let him do this though, what would she lose?

He let his other hand drift down her arm and grasped her hand. "I'll take care of you, Callie. Just let me take you home. Nothing else will happen tonight."

She swallowed hard and nodded.

She asked herself again, what else could she lose?

Everything, she thought. *Everything*.

CHAPTER SIX

Morgan was probably making a mistake, but he couldn't stop himself. Callie sat still in the passenger seat of his car, her attention on the road in front of them, rather than on him. Every once in a while she'd trace her fingers along her thigh, causing him to grip the steering wheel even harder, before she'd realize what she was doing and stop.

This was pure torture.

He'd not only been a fucking idiot at the gala when he'd judged her harshly, he'd then insisted that he'd take her home. He hoped she would forgive him for the way he'd acted at first, even if he hadn't said the cruel things aloud like others had. Though the fact that he hadn't spoken up on her behalf even quicker said it all. The fact that he was now locked in a small, enclosed space with her where her scent infiltrated his senses and made him want to pull over so he could taste every sweet inch of her didn't make things any better.

When Matt said he'd needed to leave, Morgan jumped at the chance to be alone with Callie...to take care of her. He hadn't thought twice about what that would mean—or who was listening—until it was too late. He knew he'd have to deal with Heather and his mother at some point, but he pushed it to the back of his mind for now. Their vitriol wouldn't be avoided and he'd let it roll off of him as he'd done in the past with his family and the women they put in his vicinity.

After Heather stomped off and he led Callie toward his car, he hadn't known what to say. That wasn't like him and he wasn't sure he wanted it to happen again. The woman messed up his senses and yet he wanted her to keep doing it. There was definitely something wrong with him.

She hadn't said a word when she stopped by his Audi, just raised a brow since, yes, it was the luxury model, but not one of the most expensive cars in the valet lot by far. He wasn't like the others, but he did like his comforts. After she'd rattled off her address, she faced the front window and had not spoken to him again.

He didn't know what to say or even how to breach the silence. It wasn't awkward, per se, but he would rather have figured out what they were doing next. The fact that he was taking her home, had touched her face more than once, and spoke honestly for the first time since he'd seen her told him there was no going back. Not really. She was too young for him, too innocent, but he still wanted to explore what they could have. They would have to talk.

Tonight seemed like as good a night as any.

He pulled into her driveway and turned off the car. Her home surprised him, yet he knew it shouldn't have. She lived in a small older house with neighbors close on either side; however, the trees and greenery around her property gave her a sense of privacy. She had a small porch with two chairs and a tiny table between. Her yard looked well kept, though the house looked as though it needed a fresh coat of paint. It wasn't one of the newest neighborhoods in Denver, but it wasn't a rundown area by far. She might be young, but she was clearly doing well for herself.

Even though he thought he knew enough to push her away, he clearly didn't know her at all—something that would have to change. Maybe he should listen to his gut.

"Thank you for the ride," she said softly then turned to get out of the car. He got out quicker, meeting her at the car door as she ran her hands down her dress.

"We need to talk," he said gruffly. Maybe he should have asked, rather than stated, but that wasn't the kind of man he was. He was too old to keep tiptoeing around this issue.

It wasn't fair to either of them.

She searched his gaze before nodding. "Okay. Come on in. I need to get out of these shoes anyway."

He followed her, his gaze on her bottom as he walked. He couldn't help it; she had a fantastic ass. When he walked in, he surveyed her home. The front door led to the living room, which was set off from the kitchen. Directly across from him was a hallway with three doors—probably the bathroom, and a couple of bedrooms. Everything looked like it was second-hand, well worn, but taken care of. Art covered the walls and pictures of friends and most likely family sat in frames around the living room.

"It's not much, but it's home."

He faced her and gave her a small nod. She raised her chin, but her shoulders had relaxed. "It's lovely. Truly." He thought for a moment. "It feels like you. Warm. Inviting." He wasn't always good with words, but he needed to make sure she knew that he wasn't judging. Anything but, in fact.

She looked puzzled for a moment before shaking her head. "Oh. Well, thanks." She let out a small laugh. "You always make my head fuzzy."

He smiled at that, taking one step toward her. Then another. Her eyes widened when he found himself directly in front of her.

"I like that I do that." He wanted to make her feel drunk on him, make her want more, crave more. Damn, he needed to slow it down, but he couldn't. Not then. Maybe not ever.

She closed her eyes. "You're confusing me."

"I'm confusing myself," he confessed. He let out a breath. "How old are you?" he asked, fearful of the answer.

"Twenty-five." She gave him a wry smile. "And since you yelled it at Heather, I know you're 'forty fucking years old'."

He would have laughed, but he couldn't breathe. Jesus, he'd known she was young, but hearing her actual age... "That's fifteen years."

"I can do the math, but you know what else? I'm legal. I can drink. I have decent car insurance since I hit the quarter century mark, and I own this house." She paused. "Well the bank owns most of it, but I qualified for a loan and everything since I have decent credit." Her nose wrinkled. "I'm getting off subject. If the age difference truly bothers you, then I will see you at the shop to finish your tattoo. No hard feelings."

He growled softly. Well, something was hard, and it wasn't his feelings. She seemed to read his mind because she smirked, then looked down at his crotch. Her eyes widened and he gave her a smirk of his own.

After letting out another breath, he gripped her chin and brought her gaze to his. "I want you, Callie. I'm not going to lie. I've wanted you from the moment I walked into Montgomery Ink." She opened her mouth to speak and he increased the pressure on her chin. "Let me talk first. I pushed you away and acted like an asshole more than once because, yeah, I'm older than you, and I don't think you can handle what I have to give."

She narrowed her eyes. "You won't know unless you try."

He liked her spunk. "I know. That's why we're going to risk it. You game?"

She swallowed hard and he held his breath. "I want to. You know that. I was the one who made the first move."

He ran his other hand through her hair, then wrapped it around his fist, tugging so he had better control. She let out a little gasp, her eyes darkening.

His little Callie liked that.

Good.

"Now I'm making the next. It won't be tonight, not when you've had such a tough night with us assholes, but soon, Callie. Soon."

"What do you mean? What will happen?"

He let go of her chin so he could trace her lips with his finger. Her tongue darted out and he held back a groan. He couldn't wait to have that mouth of hers on his dick.

"We're going to go slow at first, then I'm going to find out exactly what you feel like beneath me as I fuck you. I want to know more about you Callie Masters."

"I...I want that too."

"Good."

He bent down so his lips were a breath away from hers. He could feel her tremble beneath him and it revved him. Damn but he wanted her. He let his mouth brush hers twice, loving the way her breath caught with each swipe, before he kissed her fully. She moaned into his mouth, her tongue tentatively darting against his. He pulled tighter on her hair so her head was back and he had the most control. Her body sank into his and he deepened the kiss, reveling in her sweet taste.

Knowing he had to put a stop to this before they went too far, too soon, he pulled away, leaving them both panting.

"That's just a taste."

"Morgan..."

He kissed her temple, then released her. She wobbled a bit and he steadied her, cradling her to his chest.

"I'm okay," she gasped, and he smiled against her hair. He picked her up, strode toward the couch and set her down on the cushions.

"I like that you went weak-kneed for me," he said with a smug smile.

She narrowed her eyes. "I'm fine now. There's nothing weak about me."

He nodded. "I know. That's one reason I like you." He patted her knee then stood. "When I leave, lock the deadbolt behind me. I'll see you at our next appointment and then we can talk more about exactly what this entails. You understand, sweet?"

She nodded, her eyes still dark with lust.

"Good."

He left her there in her small home that smelled of her, a smile on his face.

Good.

CHAPTER SEVEN

"**Y**ou fool!"

Morgan closed his eyes, knowing this damned headache was never going to leave him. And by headache he meant his mother, not just the pounding in his temples. No amount of aspirin would shut the woman up. If he hung up, his assistant would be made to suffer. Worse, his mother would probably show up at his office once she got tired of being ignored over the phone. There were only a few things worse than a dressing down from a sixty-year-old woman in his place of business.

"What can I do for you, mother?"

"You know what you can do; you can go apologize to Heather right this very minute."

"And why would I do that?" He set his phone on his shoulder and got back to work on the documents in front of him. Just because his mother thought it was time to yell at him and call him a poor excuse for a son, didn't mean he could drop everything in order to make it happen.

Letting her yell over the phone while he barely listened seemed like the better idea. She used to drop by almost daily until he'd gotten firm with her. That had been a decade ago and, at least according to his associates, she'd only become scarier.

"Like I said, you're a fool. You're letting a perfectly good woman slip through your fingers because you can't keep your wick out of the wax."

He blinked. Huh, he wasn't sure he'd ever heard that one before. "I'm not dating Heather. The three of us knew that when I agreed to take her to the gala. In fact, I technically didn't take her. You did. I merely showed up to let her prance around me for a few hours." He winced. Now he was sounding like a cruel bastard. As much as he might not like Heather and her friends, being petty wasn't something he liked to do.

"She is the one you need to marry. I need heirs."

His mother would have been a perfect society mother in regency England. However, this was *not* that time and he was tired of her games.

"You have heirs. Lots of them. Or did you forget your daughters' children."

She huffed. "Spoiled little brats. That's what they are."

Well, he couldn't argue with her there. "I'm not marrying or having children with a woman you provide me. You haven't found a way to make me do it yet and you won't any time soon." Saying yes to Heather had been an idiotic move, but he wouldn't let it stop him from his goal.

Callie.

He could still scent her on him even though he'd showered twice since the night prior. They'd merely kissed and yet he couldn't get her out of his mind. Damn he couldn't wait to see her again.

"She is too young for you, Morgan," his mother said calmly. That didn't bode well. Whenever she was calm, that meant she was planning something that was sure to bite him in the ass later.

"She is not of your concern." He closed his eyes, his headache worsening. "The way you acted last night was a disgrace, by the way. No matter who you think you are, calling people out like that and trying to humiliate them only makes you look small. You have no right to judge."

"I have *every* right. I'll see to it that boy is ruined for bringing her into our lives."

Callie had been in his life long before that, but he needed to head this off now. "You touch Matt or anything having to do with him and I'll make you regret it."

She was silent for a moment and he ground his teeth.

"Have it your way. I won't forget this."

Neither would he.

He hung up and rubbed his eyes. Damn it. He had too much work to do, and now, he was in a piss poor mood to boot. There was no way he was getting any more work done today. After letting his surprised assistant know he was leaving early for the day, he got in his car and headed toward the city. Before he knew it, he was pulling into the Montgomery Ink parking lot rather than going home.

What the hell was he doing here? He needed to take a nap or go for a walk or something. He didn't have an appointment that day and he didn't even know if she was here. It wasn't like he and Callie were actually seeing each other. Just a promise of something to come. She wasn't there to soothe him and he damn sure knew he couldn't rely on anyone else.

The knock on his window scared the shit out of him and he turned to see Callie there.

His body immediately went hard.

He rolled down the windows and sighed. "Hey."

She smiled softly. "Hey, you're back. What's up?"

He rested his head on the back of his seat. "I don't know."

Callie leaned closer, a frown on her face. She reached out, tracing over his brow. He growled softly and reached out, gripping her wrist.

She sucked in a breath, meeting his gaze.

"You...you look like you have a headache. What's wrong?"

He kissed her fingertips then released her. She moved back out of his window and he opened the door so he could see her fully. When he reached for her again, she went down on one knee so she was at eye level with him.

"I had a headache and left early. I...I don't know why I'm here actually." He could feel his cheeks warm and he was sure he blushed. What the fuck? He did *not* blush. He didn't show weakness. As Austin once said, Morgan was one big, bad Dom. This wasn't like him.

Callie's eyes brightened and she nodded. "Okay then. I took the bus in since I worked the early shift, but if you want, I can head to your house with you." She blushed. "Just to make sure you're okay, and I can take care of that headache."

He chuckled roughly at her blush. "Oh, really?"

"Not that, you perv. Although sex does help headaches I hear. No, I'll make you eat and then give you a massage. Before I came to work here, I went to massage school so I know what I'm doing."

The idea of Callie's hands on him made him tense for an altogether new reason.

He cleared his throat. "I think I'd like that."

She smiled again. "Good. You okay to drive?"

"I think I can manage," he said dryly.

She rolled her eyes and walked around to the passenger seat. "I'm glad you came here," she said softly.

He reached out and gripped her hand. "I'm glad too."

"I still can't get over the fact that Austin has a son," Morgan said sometime later. He sat on the couch, his feet resting the coffee table with Callie by his side.

They'd been there for about an hour and they'd eaten a late lunch before relaxing in his living room. She hadn't asked about a massage yet and he wasn't sure he needed one anymore. Just being home and with Callie near him seemed to make things better. That was something he'd have to think more on later.

"I know. It's strange to think he lost so many years with Leif, but things are good now. At least I think so."

He'd wrapped his arm around her shoulders and let his fingers play with her arm, enjoying the calm way they just...sat. He was usually always on the go, a hand in at least five things at once if he could. It was nice not to have anything planned other than what *could* happen.

The two of them needed to talk about what was going on between them, but he didn't want to break the quiet peace between them. He wasn't quite sure he'd ever felt it before. She'd taken care of him like a sub would, pampering him in little ways and sighing happily when he thanked her with words and soft touches and kisses.

He wanted to see how she fit against him in all ways. There was more to him than what people saw, and he had a feeling Callie would figure that out. She wasn't high strung, but she had a tension in her body he wanted to alleviate. To do that he had to figure out how her mind worked, how she wanted to be loved, fucked, and calmed.

His groin tightened and he ran his tongue over his teeth. It seemed they needed to talk sooner rather than later or he wasn't going to last much longer.

"Have you thought about last night, little Callie?"

She turned to him, her eyes wide. He watched her reaction, the rise and fall of her chest, the way her nipples pressed against the thin top she wore. Her tongue ran along her bottom lip and it took all within him not to follow the wet trail with his own.

"Yes. A little." She blushed. "Okay, a lot. I'm not sure what you want from me though. We kind of ended everything abruptly last night."

He nodded. "True. We both needed time to think. Time to make sure it wasn't just the moment making us want to do something more."

"And...and was it?"

He tilted his head then reached out brushing her nipple with his knuckles. She sucked in a breath, and he grinned at her reaction.

"It was a promise of what is to come." This next part needed to be out in the open. He didn't want to scare her, but he might if he didn't speak up now. "Tell me, little Callie, are you as submissive as your reactions tell me?"

She blinked. "You mean submissive as in the fact you're a Dominant?"

He nodded. Good. She at least knew the idea. He'd been able to tell that she was a submissive from the first time he'd seen her, but that didn't mean she knew what it all meant.

"Yes. I'm a Dominant."

She let out a breath. "I could tell, you know. Just from the way you exude control."

He grinned then. "Good to know I haven't lost my touch." He cupped her face, letting his thumb trace her cheek. "I'm not in the scene anymore. I don't do clubs or parties or anything like that. It doesn't suit me. I'm also not into a Master/slave relationship. I like to be in control in the bedroom, but as I've gotten older, I've noticed that I don't need any of the extras that come with that." She frowned and he continued. "I don't like to inflict pain other than spankings."

Her breath caught at that and he suppressed a grin. His little Callie liked the thought of his hand on her ass. Good. "What do you like?" Over time, he would find out everything on his own through her reactions, but open communication was key.

She narrowed her eyes then nodded. "Well, everything you said is actually pretty much in line with my own wants. I don't like flogging, humiliation, or a lot of what goes on in clubs. Those kinks are great for others, but I mostly like being able to give up control and let the other person tell me what to do. That way, I can trust them enough to not only provide for my safety, but make me come the best way possible." She grinned then. "I'm not shy, despite the fact that I try not to blurt out everything I'm thinking all the time. I like it when someone ties me up because that means my other senses can open up. That doesn't mean I'll let just anyone tie me up."

He liked the fact she was so honest about her needs. The fact that those needs fit with his made it better. "We're going to have sex tonight, Callie. We both want it."

She nodded, her eyes dark with need.

"I don't want it to be just tonight though." He had to get this point across. "I don't sleep with women for just one night anymore. I'm past that." Talking about past partners might not be the best thing to do, but he needed her to understand. "When we're together, it's just us. No one else."

She swallowed hard, but relaxed at his words. "That's good because I don't share." She bit her lip and looked like she wanted to say something, but held back.

He sighed. "You need to tell me what you're thinking. Despite what people think, Doms can't read minds."

She snorted at that. "I want a relationship. I don't want everything to be just sex."

Did he want to date her and not just fuck her? Putting it like that sounded crude, and he wasn't that much of an asshole. Honestly, it hadn't occurred to him that once she gave in to him they *wouldn't* be in a full relationship.

Again, at least they were on the same page.

"I agree with you." Again, she relaxed. "Just because I want to tie you up and spank you, doesn't mean I want to use you."

She licked her lips. He had a feeling if he put his hand on her pussy right then, she'd be so fucking wet he could just slid right in. His little Callie liked the thought of what he wanted to do to her. Hell, yes.

"So we're agreed? We're moving forward?"

She rolled her eyes. "This sounds like a negotiation, not a prelude to getting naked."

He had to laugh at that. "Callie darling, this *is* a negotiation. Going forward with our eyes open keeps us safe. Speaking of safe, though we're not going to go too far into the idea of pain, I want you to use a safeword in case we go past your limits. 'Red' will do if you need me to untie you or stop spanking. 'Yellow' if I'm testing your boundaries. I might keep going though if I feel like you're blocking yourself, but that won't come until we know each other better."

She nuzzled his hand and he held back a groan. "That all sounds good." She licked her lips again. "Do you still want your massage?"

He was so fucking hard right then that if she put her hands on him, he'd spill like an inexperienced teenager. He leaned forward, brushing a soft kiss over her lips. "Next time," he whispered.

"But...but what about your headache."

He grinned. "I'm thinking we can find another way to alleviate any pressure."

She laughed softly against him. "I like the sound of that."

He stood, his body primed. When he held out a hand she put hers in his without hesitation. He nodded in appreciation and led her to his bedroom. He noticed her gaze traveled over his home and he knew at some point he should give her a proper tour. Right then, though, all he wanted to do was explore her body, not have her explore where he lived.

Her hand tightened in his as they entered his bedroom. When they made their way to the foot of the bed, he turned smiling down at her. "Are you okay, little one?"

She nodded, though he saw the hesitation in her eyes.

"Don't lie to me," he ordered without bite. "That's the worse thing you can do." He hated liars and he was grateful Callie had always been forward with him—even when it could have hurt her to do so.

"Why did you change your mind?" she asked softly.

He sighed. "I was an idiot. I thought that if I pushed you away, you'd stay away. I thought you were too young for me, too inexperienced."

She nodded. "I'm not that young. Fifteen years means nothing when it comes to who I am now. And I'm more experienced than I look."

He trailed his hand down her arm. He didn't want to think about who she'd been with before, but the fact that she'd done at least some of the things he'd wanted to do to her meant he hopefully wouldn't scare her. She was woman enough to handle him and that was all that mattered. He purposely put the thoughts of a future and what it would mean if they were together for longer than a breath out of his mind. They were just starting out and worrying about what might happen if they became truly serious would only hurt them.

Instead he cupped the back of her head and kissed her. Hard. He tangled his tongue with hers, fucking her mouth as he soon would her pussy. She moaned into him and he cupped her breast with his other hand. She gasped and he let the weight fill his palm. He couldn't wait to see the color of her nipples, taste them. She was so damn responsive that he wanted to find out if she could come by playing with her tits alone.

He had a feeling she would...and she'd love it.

He pulled away, leaving her panting, her lips swollen from his kisses. Next time, they would be swollen from sucking his cock. He held back a groan at the thought of her on her knees, his hand in her hair as he held her still while he fucked her mouth, spilling down her throat. That would have to wait until next time. Tonight he wanted to please her, make her come over and over again until she was too spent to move.

"Strip," he ordered once he got himself under control.

She didn't hesitate to pull her shirt off her head. Fuck. Yes. This little sub would be perfect for him. He knew it.

He folded his arms over his chest, his gaze on her as she moved in sensual, fluid motion. She undid her pants, sliding them down her legs. That left her in a lacy bra that didn't cover much and a thong that sat low on her hips.

She looked up at him expectantly and he frowned. "Strip all the way, little Callie."

She nodded and unhooked her bra. The cups fell forward and she caught them before tossing the whole thing on the ground.

Fucking. Perfect.

He held himself in check so he wouldn't touch her. It wasn't time.

Her tits were a perfect handful, not too big, not too small. He was a tit man, but he didn't need size to get off. No, he needed responsiveness. The cool air in the room, and he hoped his presence, caused her nipples to tighten into hard little pink peaks. Her breasts were high, round, and begging for his mouth.

Soon, he told himself. Soon.

When she wiggled out of her thong, he held his breath. Her bare pussy looked freshly waxed, glistening at the juncture from her arousal.

She stood there, her head high as he studied her. He held up one finger then made a motion for her to turn. She smiled and he held back a laugh. His little Callie liked the attention. When she turned, he licked his lips at the sight of her. She wasn't skinny, but she wasn't too round either. She had just the right curves, and the ink on her body only highlighted her toned muscles and shape.

She stopped so her back was completely to him and he grunted in approval. He stepped toward her, making sure he moved with enough noise that he wouldn't startle her. Before he touched her, he stood still, loving the way her body tightened in anticipation of his touch.

He traced her shoulder with his finger and she shivered.

"You look beautiful, Callie," he whispered. She sighed, and he moved his other hand around to cup her breast. She arched her back pressing her nipple into his palm so he pulled back. "Don't move, darling. Be a good girl and let me touch you."

She sucked in a breath and he smiled. His hands explored her body, soft touches over softer skin. She sighed and gasped as he cupped her breasts again, plucking her nipples. When he pulled her back to his front, pressing his covered erection against the crack of her ass, they both moaned.

"You're such a good girl." He nibbled on her ear. She didn't move, though her body shook. "What do you want, baby girl? You need to say the words."

"I...I want to touch you."

He smiled, nipping at her neck. "What else?"

"I want to come. Please, Morgan...should I call you Sir?"

He kicked at her right foot gently forcing her legs to spread. "I want you to call me Morgan." He paused. "Actually, you can call me Morgan or, like you did in the shop, Mr. McAllister. I liked when you were bratty to me then, but know that if you're too bratty, I will punish you."

"Okay, Morgan."

"Good girl. Now keep your legs spread." He palmed her ass, squeezing and molding the globes before running his finger down the crack. She shivered as he tapped her puckered hole. "Do you want my cock in your ass?"

He had one hand on her neck so he could feel her swallow hard though he couldn't see her eyes. He'd turn her soon so he could see each and every reaction.

"I've had decent anal sex before, but never anything earth shattering," she answered.

He swatted her bottom twice in quick succession. She let out a little scream and he grinned at the rosy marks he'd left. She'd redden nicely.

"Don't compare me to other men, little Callie. I asked you if you wanted my cock in your ass."

"Yes, Mr. McAllister."

Damn, but he liked the sound of that. He continued his exploration of her body, running his fingers through her drenched folds.

"You're so fucking wet. I can't wait to eat this pussy of yours. Do you want that? Do you want my mouth on your cunt, eating and licking up every inch of you?"

"God yes. Please. Please eat me."

He grinned and moved back. She whimpered, so he turned her in his arms. "Don't worry, Callie, I won't leave you wanting for too long." He crushed his mouth to hers, unable to wait any longer. She arched into him and he let her, knowing that he'd have her writhing even more for him soon.

He walked her backwards toward his bed, eager, wanting, craving. When he pulled away, she reached for him, trying to kiss him again. He gripped her small wrists in one hand and gently raised them over her head.

The position forced her tits out and arched her back.

Such a fucking beautiful pose.

"I want you to grip the bedpost behind you. Can you do that?"

"What are you going to do to me?" she asked, breathless.

He raised a brow. "I asked you a question, sub."

She swallowed and nodded.

"Out loud, Callie."

"Yes, yes I can do that."

"Show me."

She wrapped her hands around the bedpost while she licked her lips.

"Nice. Now if I eat that pretty cunt of yours, are you going to be able to keep your arms up? If not, I can tie you up right now. In fact, I am going to do that sometime. Let me know if you'll be a good girl and do it yourself right now."

"I'll be good. I promise."

She looked so open, so earnest, and he couldn't help but cup her face and kiss her softly. "I know, honey. You're trying so hard. I'm going to reward you."

"Please."

He kissed her again and trailed his lips over her neck, her shoulders, then down between her breasts. He sucked on each nipple, pulling back once they were red, aching. She moaned, wiggling against the bedpost, but not letting go. Then he moved down her belly, laving at her belly button before kneeling before her. He spread her legs so he could take his fill.

"So fucking wet, Callie. You're sopping." He trailed his finger over her clit, loving the whimpers escaping from her mouth, then rubbed along her labia. He pulled away, his finger covered in her juices. When he met her gaze, he licked his finger clean, groaning at her sweet taste. "Like peaches," he whispered.

He spread her wider, running his thumbs along her pussy. Then he leaned down and latched onto her clit, sucking and scraping his teeth along the hood, before lapping her up. He ran two fingers along her slit then entered her, curling his fingers so he found her G-spot.

She shook, but again, didn't let go.

"Morgan, oh God, Morgan. I'm going to come. Please. Please let me come."

Jesus, he loved the fact she asked. She wanted his permission and that above all else told him it was time to let her come so he could be inside her.

He rubbed his finger along the sensitive bundle of nerves and looked up. "Come."

She met his gaze and shattered. Her eyes going glassy as she arched her back. Her fingers turned white where she gripped the bedpost.

She didn't let go.

He fucked her with his fingers, pumping in and out of her as hard as he could without hurting her, letting her come down from her release. When she stopped shaking, he pulled out and stood up.

"Bend over the bed, little Callie."

She nodded, her body rosy pink from her orgasm.

"First," he said, then kissed her, taking each mewl and moan as his success. "Can you taste yourself on me?"

"Yes."

"You like it?"

"Only on you," she said softly and Morgan groaned.

Jesus, he couldn't get enough of her. "Bend over, baby."

While she did, he quickly pulled off his clothes, and got the condom out of his wallet. The next time he took her, he'd use the ones from his nightstand. He rolled it over his length then walked toward her.

"You look perfect bent over in front of me, Callie."

She wiggled her ass, drawing a laugh out of him. He smacked her bottom and she gasped. "That hurt," she said as she looked over her shoulder.

"Did I tell you that you could look at me?" he asked, then smacked her other cheek. He ran his hands over her, taking out the sting.

"I'm sorry, Mr. McAllister."

"You want my cock, baby?"

"Please, Morgan. Please, fuck me."

He smiled at her begging then gripped her hips. The bed was at just the right height so that he didn't have to do any fancy maneuvering in order to slide right into her heat. First, though, he cupped her sex.

"You're so fucking hot, Callie. You're wet, ready, and willing. I'm going to fuck you hard, fuck you until neither of us can think. Then, when we're ready, I'm going to make slow love to you, and watch you come as you grip my cock, milking me until we're both spent."

"I love that you're a dirty talker."

He grinned. "Just you wait and see." He positioned himself at her entrance and slowly entered her. They both groaned at the feeling. "Jesus, you're fucking tight."

"I think it's the fact that you're fucking big."

He chuckled. "You're a smart ass, but thank you for the compliment." Sweat trickled down his back and the cords on his neck stood out, but he had to go slow until she grew accustomed to his girth. He didn't want to hurt her.

When he was all the way in, he paused, trying to gauge her. "You okay, little one?"

"Uh huh," she said, her voice strained. "I need you to move though. Please, for the love of God, move. I want you to fuck me, Morgan. I'm not fine china. I won't break."

He slapped her ass again and was rewarded with her cunt clamping around his dick. "Tone, girl. Watch it."

"Then fuck me," she snapped.

He smacked her again then moved. He pulled out slowly, then pummeled back into her. His balls tightened and he cursed. No, he wouldn't come so quickly, not now. Not ever. He couldn't help it that Callie was one hot piece of everything he thought he'd never have.

He set a grueling pace, keeping them both panting. Her hands dug into the comforter and he knew she was close. "Come one more time, baby."

She arched her back and he thrust upward so she could come. When she screamed his name, he pulled out and flipped her on her back. Before she could catch her breath, he had her legs spread and was fucking her again.

"Jesus, Morgan. Oh, my God."

He met her sex-drunk gaze, and growled. "Mine, Callie. Do you understand? You're mine."

"Yours," she panted.

He put her legs on his shoulders and bent her so that he could reach her lips in a bruising kiss, all the while sliding in and out of her sweet cunt. Thank the gods she was so flexible. He was going to have fun with her.

"Morgan," she gasped then opened her mouth in a scream, coming once more around his dick. He couldn't take it anymore and followed her, filling the condom quickly. Damn, he was pretty sure he'd come so hard, he'd overfill the damn thing if he wasn't careful.

When they slowed, he didn't want to pull out of her, so instead he used the last of his strength to push her up on the bed while he was still deep inside her.

"You feel so good around my cock, Callie," he whispered, kissing down her jaw. He rolled her nipples between his fingers, just wanting to touch her.

Her hands slowly ran up his back and down again. "I don't think I'm going to be able to move for a week."

He kissed her again. "Good."

She smiled and he knew he was lost. Damn, he didn't know what would come of the two of them, nor did he know what he wanted to happen. What he did know was that he liked her in his arms, in his bed.

Now he just needed to figure out what to do with what he felt.

Or rather, put a name to those feelings in the first place.

CHAPTER EIGHT

Was there such a thing as too much sex? Callie didn't think so. She sat gingerly down on the stool at her station and held back a wince. Okay, so maybe there was such a thing as too much sex. Flashes of how well she'd been taken care of the night before filled her mind and she blushed. When he'd bent her over that table and showed her *exactly* how bad a girl she'd been...well, her ass still showed the marks.

She and Morgan had been together for two weeks and had been together each night. Half of the nights they did nothing more than eat out and cuddle, but it was something.

She would say they'd gone from zero to sixty in a flash, but in all honesty, they weren't spending *that* much time together. Between her new clients and his job, they only had a few hours here and there. Instead of getting downtime, she spent it with Morgan, getting to know him and how they worked together. It wasn't like they had keys to each other's places yet. Sure, she'd met his mother, but that was a whole other matter all together.

Meeting another's parents shouldn't include dirty names and judgments. Well, on second thought, that *could* be what happened with others, but not necessarily what Callie wanted when it came to a relationship with anyone.

She shook her head. Nope, she wasn't going to go there. She didn't want to think about expectations and people she wanted to stay away from. Instead, she'd focus on her art, herself, and enjoying her time with Morgan.

Today though, she'd see him again and not just for making her hot. This time he was coming in for more of the work on his back and then she'd work on the outlines on his arms. Those she knew would hurt more than the others he'd had so far. In fact, he'd been stoic and seemed comfortable during their previous session. This time for his ink would be the first time she'd have her hands on him professionally since she'd had her hands on him in the yummy, sweaty kind of way.

"What is that hip shake for?" Morgan asked from behind her and she jumped, her hand over her heart.

She turned, blushing at being caught dancing. Again. Considering she hadn't even known she'd been doing a little hip shake at the thought of getting naked with the man in front of her, she felt her cheeks heat up even more.

"You scared the crap out of me," she said, trying not to sound so breathless. This was just Morgan, why was she acting like she hadn't seen him in years? In fact, she'd left his bed that morning so she could get to work. He was already up and dressed by the time she got ready and she was fine with that. Normally they didn't have shower sex since that tended to take up so much time they both ended up running late, so she hadn't missed it that morning.

He cocked his head, his lips twitching. Damn she loved his expressions. He never tried to be too open, too exuberant, but the small touches made it for her. She probably shouldn't have thought things like that because it brought her one step closer to falling in love with the man, but she couldn't help it.

They hadn't discussed whether they were serious or not, nor had they talked about the future. Why would they? It had only been a couple of weeks and they were still getting to know one another, but the idea of something more with him than just right now started to settle over her.

She was only in her mid twenties, and most of her friends her age weren't ready to settle down and think about having only one person in their lives until the end. That didn't mean she never thought about what it would be like to be married and have children, but it had never really been on her radar. Not seriously anyway.

Damn though, it wasn't as if she was really thinking of Morgan that way. They hadn't even been dating for a month yet so she wasn't about to picture a ring on her finger and a baby in her belly. She was so not ready for that, but for some reason she *was* ready to think past the next month when it came to a man in her life

Scary.

Morgan cupped her face and she blinked up at him. Damn, she must have been lost in her own thoughts while he stared at her.

"You okay, Callie?"

She nodded and he shook his head.

"Words, little Callie. I need to hear your words. I've asked you if you were okay three times now and you've been in your own little world. What's wrong, girl?"

She leaned into his palm and sighed. Was it wrong that she loved when he called her girl or little Callie? To her, it meant he cared even though they had the age difference that might bother others. There was nothing wrong with fifteen years and since she was enjoying herself, she should just live it to the fullest.

"I'm okay," she said honestly. "Just thinking and apparently being a bad girlfriend."

She froze. Girlfriend? Damn it. It wasn't like they were in high school and Morgan was far from that point. Nowhere had they used those terms and now she'd just blurted it out.

Morgan smiled and lowered his head, brushing his lips over hers. Her body relaxed immediately, turning into a pool of Callie at his touch alone.

"If something is bothering you and I don't know about it, that makes me a bad boyfriend."

The little cheerleader inside her head did a little happy dance. *He likes me, he really likes me.* Okay, Sally Field, that's enough of that.

Relieved she hadn't made a mistake with the careless use of a word that could mean so much, she pulled back and stood on her toes. She kissed his chin and his eyes warmed.

"Honestly, I'm good. Just being an airhead. So...you want to get started?" She ran her hands over his broad shoulders and down his arms. So. Freaking. Sexy. "I can't wait to get my hands on you."

"You just want to get me naked," he whispered.

She blushed harder and licked her lips.

He growled low and leaned down to bite her bottom lip. Her toes curled and she cleared her throat. While it would be fan-freaking-tastic to make out with him and taste every inch of him, she was fully aware they were in the middle of the shop.

She could practically feel Sloane's and Austin's gazes bore into her back. Yeah, probably not the best place to show so much affection when she was supposed to be working on Morgan's ink, not his kink.

"Get a room!" Maya called from her side and Callie snorted. Trust Maya to break the moment.

Callie turned on her heel and put her hands on her hips. "Excuse me. I have my own little cubby right here." She used her fingers to make a box around her. "That's a room."

Sloane huffed a laugh. "Maybe get one with walls next time if you're going to heat up the shop with just a hello." He smiled as he said it and Callie relaxed. She'd been worried that her friends—*family*—would be worried or at least a little judgmental about her and Morgan, but she shouldn't have been. At least from what she saw, they were okay with it, if albeit a little overprotective, but they were like that with any man she brought by.

Morgan's arm came around her waist and settled over her hip, his fingers playing with the peek of skin between her top and short skirt. Her knees trembled and she bit her lip. Damn the man's touch alone made her want to come.

So not the place for it considering she had to work on his back and arms today.

"Okay crew, get back to your work. I'm going to do mine."

Austin raised a brow even as he kept his needle on his client. "Sure honey, you go do that." He grinned and she rolled her eyes.

Boys.

She turned again and looked up at Morgan. "Okay, strip."

He raised a brow of his own but she held firm. "Isn't that usually my line?" he asked softly.

Not too softly since Sloane laughed behind her.

Boys. Again.

"Hey, you want ink? You strip." She leaned closer. "And if you're a good boy I'll be a bad girl for you in this skirt of mine," she whispered.

Morgan scowled then leaned even closer. "You know how uncomfortable it's going to be sitting with a fucking hard-on while you work on me?"

She smiled. "Then we better get to work."

He undid the buttons on his shirt and stripped it off. She swallowed hard, forcing herself to pull her gaze—and her hands—away from his firm chest and lickable abs. It wasn't fair that he could look so good and she had to be good as well. Only the promise of being oh-so-bad later made this worth it. Well, that and the fucking kickass ink he would be getting by hers truly.

Her fingers itched to trace the little star burst on his hip but she refrained. She could play with the lines of ink on his back since she was the one who put them there and would be adding more today, but playing with his hips and having her hand near his dick wouldn't help either of them.

"I know where your mind is going, girl; keep it clean," Morgan growled softly. "For now."

She smiled and rolled her eyes. "Sit facing the other way. I have all my stuff ready for you but I want to check out how my work looks on you since our last session."

He straddled the chair but looked over his shoulder at her. "Didn't you do that last night?"

"Shut up. We're at work so now I'm doing it again."

He turned back and she held back a sigh at his back. Damn the man had definition, plus her ink, hell yeah. He'd taken great care of her work—it helped that she'd been with him for all of it, caring for each inch of that magnificent back of his. She'd taught him how to use a spatula to get the hard to reach places with ointment if she couldn't do it herself. An old trick, but hey, it worked. She liked it better, though, when she could soothe his aches herself.

Knowing the others would be watching her, she carefully traced over the edges of her last session, getting a feel for what she would be doing today. She forced herself not to sigh or spend too much time in one place. She wasn't afraid she'd swoon all over him once she got started since the buzz of the needle helped her focus, but right then, she needed to clear her head.

"Okay, I'm going to work on finishing the outline on your back and do your arms. If we're still feeling good pain-wise, then I will start on your coloring." She tilted her head, her mind calculating every movement and arch of his back. "We should be able to get to some of the coloring done since your skin takes ink so well and you don't move." Having to stop over and over when her client flinched or got restless made for a long night, but Morgan was a trooper. Plus, she was planning on rewarding him for his efforts later.

He looked over his shoulder at her again and smiled. Damn, her heart thumped. He had to quit looking at her like that or she was going to fall for him. She couldn't afford to do that, not when she wasn't sure what he really wanted when it came to them. Frankly, she wasn't sure what she wanted either. It was a recipe for disaster if she didn't hold back.

Morgan's smile slid off his face. "What's wrong, Callie?"

She shook her head, putting on a bright smile. "Nothing. I'm just thinking about where I'm going to start," she lied. No use worrying him and end up scaring him away. "Ready?"

He nodded, his brows low, then turned.

She let out a sigh and got to work. After she cleaned his skin, she let the buzz of the needle soothe her worries. Morgan never moved or grunted, even as she worked the delicate parts of his arm and near his wrists. After two hours of bending over his back, working on the intricate feathers of the phoenix's wings, she sat up and got him something to drink from the fridge. Knowing her man, he probably could have gone longer without a break, but she didn't need to push either of them.

He smiled at her when she gave him his juice and she had to hold back from kissing him. When the needle had been moving, it was easy to turn off the emotion and act professional, but as soon as she looked into his eyes, the emotions flared again. Thankfully, he didn't speak, but held out his free hand and gripped hers.

"Ready to go again?"

"Yep. Afterwards, you want to eat at my place and stay the night?"

She bit her lip and nodded. She wanted that more than anything, but she wasn't about to act needy. Damn it, what was wrong with her? This wasn't like her and she didn't like what the insecurities were doing to her.

"Let's do a couple more hours and finish up your arms. After that we'll see where you're at and try and get some coloring in. If we don't end up doing that tonight, it's no big deal. We have a couple more sessions ahead of us anyway."

"We need to stop by your place for clothes?" he asked, then drained his juice.

"No, I have a bag in my car." She winced. "I keep it in there just in case. It wasn't like I was presuming."

Morgan cupped her face and she told herself not to pull back. "Hey, don't worry. I like that you have your things ready." He grinned. "I have a bag too, just in case you wanted me at your place. It's easier than tip toeing, baby."

She sighed then straightened. "Good. Now let's get to work on your other arm. You'll tell me if you're in too much pain right?" She glared at him. "Don't act all macho if you need a break."

He snorted then pointed to his back. "I'm good, baby. Beside, you know my body well enough that you'll be able to tell if I'm in pain."

That was true. She knew every single inch of him and enjoyed it all. The fact he knew that and knew her body just as well made it feel like it was okay that she wanted more.

At least she hoped so.

By the time they finished up their part of the night, another three hours had passed and she was ready for a break herself. Morgan was a trouper, but she knew he had reached his limit. She cleaned up his back and went over aftercare instructions again. It didn't matter that they'd just done this and she would be going home with him to take care of him herself, she wouldn't forget to explain what needed to be done to keep her work in top form.

They said their goodbyes to the rest of the crew at Montgomery Ink and headed out to their cars. Morgan walked her to her door, leaning down to kiss her softly.

"See you at my place?" he asked, a promise in his eyes that left her breathless.

"Yes, but are you sure you're up for...gymnastics?"

He grinned, cupped her chin. "I'll be on top this time, then."

"Aren't you usually on top?" she teased, loving the touch of his skin on hers.

"You like it, girl. You want me to pick up something for dinner? Or scrounge around in the fridge?"

"We have leftovers in your fridge from the café I took you to, so we can just munch on that." They'd gone to a hippie café that she loved for organic sandwiches and the best soup she'd ever tasted. Morgan had fit right in though he probably made in a week what some of the people there made in a year. He hadn't looked down at the clientele or the worn tables and chairs. It made her want him even more. Yes, he'd taken her to a fancy French restaurant—complete with table linens and no prices on the menu—but she hadn't felt uncomfortable. In fact, just being with him made her feel better. If people looked at them like being with him was an issue, she hadn't noticed it—although she hadn't seen anyone from the gala there, including his mother and that blonde waif—so it could have been a fluke. Either way, they were both showing where they'd come from and how easily the other could fit in when it came to dating. It meant something and she wasn't going to take anything for granted.

"Sounds like a plan. I might have to go back soon for more of their soup." He traced her jaw and she shivered.

"I'll take you," she said back then pulled away. "Now, drive safe and I will see you soon."

He said goodbye with a kiss and she got in her car. He wouldn't move until she was safely locked in her vehicle, so there was no use waiting to watch him walk away so she could get a good look at his ass. She'd do that once they got to his place. Twice.

By the time they made it to his place and finished eating, she had her shoes off and her feet tucked under her as she leaned into Morgan. She had to be careful since his arms and back were covered in new ink, but he must still have been on the adrenaline and endorphin high since he didn't seem bothered.

"So, you said if I behaved at the shop, you'd be a very, very bad girl for me," Morgan said softly and she shivered, her pussy tightening. She winced and he pulled away. "What's wrong, baby?"

She wasn't about to lie to him since that wasn't how they worked, plus her aching for a different reason than the need to come didn't sound like something she needed to deal with. "We've been having so much sex recently, I think my pussy needs a break."

His eyes widened and he slid his hand down her back, over her ass, so he cupped her. She sucked in a breath as he patted her softly. It didn't hurt, but she was tender.

"Poor baby. I've been rough with you."

She shook her head. "No, well, maybe, but I've liked it. You didn't do anything I haven't wanted and I want you more tonight." She let out a breath and lowered her gaze. "So, maybe we can do something else tonight that doesn't involve your dick in my cunt?"

He growled softly. "Those dirty words coming out of that sweet little mouth make me so fucking hard, Callie girl." He tucked his other hand under her chin and forced her gaze to his. "We won't make love tonight like we have been."

Make love.

No, she wouldn't think about that. Not when she was a mess as it was.

"I want to fuck your ass, Callie. What do you say? I know you like it when I play with that little hole and we've been preparing you with the different plugs. You think you're ready?"

She licked her lips, her body tight and ready. "I want that."

"Want what, Callie? Tell me."

"I want you to fuck my ass."

"Good girl."

He kissed her then, softly at first, then ramping up until she moaned into him, his tongue fucking her mouth. She wanted to run her hands all over him but stopped herself before she hurt his new ink. Tonight would be hard not to go too fast, too rough, but she wanted him. Now.

Morgan pulled away. "Go to the bedroom, put on those fuck me shoes you left in my closet, and bend over the bed. You said you've been a bad girl so I'm going to ruck up that little pleated skirt of yours and spank you until your ass is bright red. Then I'm going to fill that little hole with my cock so I can fuck you hard. You ready, girl?"

132

Her nipples tightened and her pussy ached for him—even though he wouldn't be filling her there that night.

"Callie?"

She sucked in a breath. "I'm ready."

"Go to the bedroom. Be ready when I get there or I'll have to punish you."

She scurried away, her body shaking with excitement. They didn't go kinky every night because neither of them needed it all the time, but when they did...dear God she loved it.

Once she got her shoes out of his closet— the fact that they were there in the first place was something she'd have to contemplate later—she wobbled to the bed and bent over. Damn. Was she supposed to keep her panties on or take them off? Knowing how her man liked her ready, she quickly shimmied out of them, aware that he could be in at any moment and if she wasn't ready she'd be punished.

She shivered at the thought.

Oh yeah, she was demented, but she was *his* demented girl.

Bare and ready for him, she bent over the bed, placing her cheek on the mattress. She arched her back so her ass was up, her cheeks spread slightly.

She could only see part of the door out of the corner of her eye, so she closed them, knowing the anticipation would be worth it. She heard him shuffle inside and knew he'd made noise so he wouldn't startle her.

God, she could love this man.

Stop it, Callie.

"Such a good girl," Morgan whispered before running his hand down her back.

She shivered and wiggled her ass.

He slapped her bottom hard and she froze.

"Don't move, little Callie. You're mine to feast on, mine to play with. You don't move until I tell you."

She swallowed hard, but didn't open her eyes. She would if he told her to but right now she wanted to feel everything, know he was there for her...would always be there for her.

He ran his hands down her legs, his fingers massaging her, leaving her aching. Her legs wobbled in her heels and he gripped her thighs.

"You look fucking hot in these heels baby, but I don't want you to hurt yourself. You okay with them on while I take in my feel?"

She nodded.

He spanked her again.

"Use your words."

"Yes, Morgan. I'm okay. I like the way I look for you."

"Good girl."

He rucked up her skirt and the coolness of the room brushed the heat of her pussy.

"You took off your panties."

"Was that okay?"

He cupped her and she gasped. "Better than okay. I didn't tell you what to do and the fact you made yourself ready for me makes me happy, Callie." His knuckle ran down her folds and she shivered. "I know you're tender baby so I we'll let this pretty pussy have a rest tonight. You okay with me sucking on your clit?

I'll be gentle but I want you to be able to come and we don't know if you'll come from me in your ass yet."

"That sounds good," she said on a breath. "Good."

He smacked her right cheek and she groaned. The sting ached something fierce, but then he'd blow on it or rub her softly so the pain fell into pleasure. He smacked her other side then repeated the process, never fully hitting the same spot twice. Her body arched, begging for more like the kinky girl she was.

"Come, Callie. Can you come with just my hand?"

She moaned and let the pain send her over the edge. Her body shook and she let out a breath as she came down. She wasn't a pain slut or a full masochist, but the fact that Morgan wanted her to come sent her over the edge.

Apparently her addiction centered around the intense, sexy man behind her.

Perfect.

Morgan ran his hands over her back and ass, before he caressed her neck. He leaned over her and kissed her hard.

"Your ass is so fucking red, baby. I love the way you color. You ready for me to fuck you, baby girl?"

She nodded then licked her lips. "Yes, please. Please fill me."

He grinned and then she reached out, gripping the part of his wrist she hadn't tattooed yet.

"What is it, little Callie?"

"I want to taste you. Can I?" She loved giving him blowjobs because while she was the one who gave him pleasure, he was the one who controlled her. Damn, she loved it all.

He grinned, then stood up. "You want your mouth on my dick? Fuck yeah." When he held out a hand, she put her in his and stood. "Let's take off those shoes so you don't hurt your ankles."

"Won't I be on my knees?"

"Cheeky. I like it. You want me naked while you blow me?"

"You want me to decide?"

He cupped her face and met her gaze. "I want you to have anything you want, Callie girl."

She swallowed hard, her heart swelling. "Take off your clothes. I want to see your ink, and I want to have all of you in my mouth—or at least all I can fit."

He nodded then, knelt at her feet. She sucked in a breath as he carefully took off her shoes, sliding his hands up her legs so he could cup her tender ass. He kissed her belly and stood again, stripping off his clothes.

When he finished, he stood there naked, peeks of his link coming over his arms since she hadn't finished yet. His cock slapped his belly, leaving a trail of wetness in its wake.

"You won't be able to suck me down for too long, darling. I'm a little close to the trigger right now and I want to fill that pretty ass of yours."

He held out a hand and she took it to steady herself as she knelt before him.

His hand tangled in her hair and she looked up at him. "You look so beautiful on your knees."

"Brute," she teased.

"Your brute."

She warmed and licked the underside of his cock.

"Fuck, that feels so good."

She smiled and licked him again, sucking on the tip of his cock before taking as much of him as she could. She hollowed out her cheeks as she pulled away then rolled his balls in her hands. His hand kept her head steady and she opened her mouth wider, letting him fuck her at his pace, loving the way he kept in control. Her gaze never left the starburst tattoo on his stomach because she could watch the way the thick muscles of his body worked as he strained for control.

He pulled away and she whimpered. "Shirt off. Bra off. Then lay face down on the bed." He kissed her hard. "You're so good at that, baby, but I want to save myself for your ass."

She smiled and did as she was told. He went to the nightstand drawer, covered his cock with a condom then started to lube himself up. Damn, but he was big. This was going to hurt, but she trusted him to make it good for the both of them.

"I'm going to put a pillow under your hips so I have a better angle. And as much I want to have you face me so I can see your face as you come, this will be better for you for the first time. Next time I'm in your ass, we'll do it face-to-face. Okay?"

"Anything, Morgan. I trust you."

His eyes brightened and he leaned down to kiss her. "You have no idea what it means to me to hear you say that."

"Yes. I do."

He let out a breath, kissed her again then climbed onto the bed behind her. He ran his hands up and down her ass, molding her cheeks in his large hands.

"You're still so pink, Callie. Your pussy is glistening and ready. I won't play with that tender area tonight, but I will be stroking your clit to make you come. I know I already said that, but I wanted to make sure you were still ready for it."

She wiggled her ass, more than ready. "I am. Please, Morgan. Please fuck my ass."

"As my girl wants." He started to work on preparing her using one finger, then two, slowly lubing her up, playing with her puckered hole. Her muscles tightened, but his hand on her clit made her relax and let more of him in. By the time he had three fat fingers in her, she was panting.

"I think you're ready for me, but let me know everything you're feeling. Are you ready, Callie?"

"I'm ready," she whispered.

The head of his cock pressed against her entrance and she forced herself not to tense up.

"Relax baby, and push out. It will make it easier."

She did so and she felt him fill her. The pressure was so freaking much and she wanted to shout out, but instead she took a deep breath, letting Morgan's soothing whispers and touches make it all better. When he was fully in her, he rested there for a moment, his fingers running over her swollen clit.

"You feel so fucking good, Callie. I'm going to blow just sitting here. You okay, honey?"

"Uh huh. I need you to move...do something. I'm so full."

"Anything you want, Callie. Anything you need."

Then he moved. She arched up, needing to be as close as possible to him as he made love to her. He pumped in and out of her, keeping one hand on her clit and the other stroking up and down her side before eventually reaching her chin. He leaned over her and took her mouth. His taste pushed her over the edge and she came hard against him. When he pulled back and shouted, she could feel him filling the condom deep within her.

She lay gasping, trying to catch her breath as he pulled out. Boneless, she lay there as he disposed of the condom, then came back with a warm washcloth to clean her up. He was so gentle, so caring that she couldn't help the tears streaking down her cheeks.

"Shh, sweet Callie, I've got you," he whispered when he was done. He pulled her into his arms, wrapped them both in the covers and held her close. "Let it out, baby."

She snuggled into him, inhaling his scent, never wanting to let him go.

She loved him.

Loved him so much and yet she knew if she said anything, it would be too soon.

He rested his cheek on the top of her head and sighed. "Sleep, Callie mine. I'll be here when you wake."

Trusting him to not let her go, she closed her eyes.

She'd deal with her feelings, her future, all of that in the morning. For right now, she was content in his arms, in his bed, and in his life.

That's all she could ask for.

At least for now.

CHAPTER NINE

The buzz of the needle soothed Callie as she worked on her latest client of the day. It had been three days since she realized she loved Morgan and yet she wasn't the least bit stressed. It was as if her mind and body had finally aligned and she was ready for the next step. She might be younger than him, but she knew her mind.

She also didn't need to get married, have kids, and have the so-called perfect life right away. A future didn't have to be on one path and as long as she could eventually reveal her feelings, then she'd be okay. The thought of getting married and having kids didn't scare her anymore, but she was nowhere near ready for that.

The idea that she could also crave Morgan's collar as well didn't scare her. That, though, was something else she'd have to eventually think about.

At the moment, her mind was on her client and the final shading of the kickass skull tattoo on his calf. There was so much she could do to the traditional skull tattoo to make it unique to the wearer. She was a fan of all ink as long as it made the person happy.

She finished up, went over the aftercare instructions and walked her client out. He tipped her amazingly well and she did another hip shake.

"You and that dancing thing of yours," Sloane said from behind her and she yelped.

She turned on her heel and put her fists on her hips. "What is it with everyone coming up behind me and scaring the crap out of me." The words 'coming up behind' made her blush and Sloane raised a brow.

"Oh no. I don't want to know what that blush is for." He held up his hands and walked away slowly. "Whatever kinky shit you and the old man get up to does *not* need to be on my brain."

"Aww, you only wish you could get as kinky as our girl, Callie," Maya said from her station.

Callie flipped her off and waved at Maya's seventy-year old client. "Sorry, Mrs. Peterman."

"It's okay honey. I like knowing that you young ones are actually using that libido of yours. In fact, Mr. Peterman and I used to get down right dirty when we were in public." She sighed. "Oh, the things he used to love to do to me on the hood of his Chevy."

Brain.

Bleach.

"Good for you, Mrs. Peterman," Maya said with a smile.

Callie shook her head and followed Sloane to his station where he was letting his client rest for a moment. She held back a gasp at the intricate work on the man's skin. It was the perfect eagle that represented everything he—and Sloane—had fought for when they'd risked their lives countless times. It looked as if she could reach out and touch its feathers.

"It looks great," she whispered and Sloane smiled softly, then got back to work.

The older man in the chair smiled as well, and she walked away quietly, giving the two of them space. This was why she loved ink. It brought people together, helped heal, and spoke of memories and forever.

She didn't want to do anything else.

"Hey, Callie, you okay?" Austin asked as he came up to her side.

She smiled at him, wrapping an arm around his waist. He did the same to her shoulder and she settled. "I'm doing great, actually. Sloane is kicking butt over there and I just did some awesome ink. I'm happy."

Austin met her gaze and frowned. "Is it only the ink making you happy?"

"Huh?"

"You and Morgan—you two doing okay?"

Why was he asking? "Why wouldn't we be okay?"

He shrugged, but didn't let her go. "When I wanted you to do his ink, I hadn't thought you'd two would get together as well."

Annoyed, she narrowed her eyes. "Are you saying I'm not good enough for him?"

Austin backed up. "Whoa. What the fuck, Callie? Why would you think I'd think that?"

"I don't know Austin, you're the one who brought it up." Hurt, she folded her arms over her chest.

"No, I only said I didn't think you'd hook up with him. He's older and the both of you come from different worlds."

"So the fuck what?"

"Hey, you two, stop fighting."

"Back off, Maya," they snapped at the same time.

"Fine, but be honest with the each other and stop jumping to conclusions. Both of you," Maya snapped then went back to work.

"Callie. You're like my little sister. I love you. You know that. I think that the two of you work. It didn't cross my mind that it would even be a thing at first, but now that I see it. Cool. But I don't know everything going on, and since I'm that big brother of yours, I'm going to pry to make sure my girl is treated right. Okay?"

Callie relaxed and immediately felt like bitch. "I'm sorry. I...I don't know why I reacted the way I did."

"I think that you have things you need to figure out with him. I know the two of you haven't fully figured out the future or one of you would have mentioned it."

"We're still new," she said softly.

Austin hugged her close. "I know, baby doll. And I'm prying because I love you. I want you to be happy."

"I am." She *was*. Only she hadn't fully figured out how she would fit in his life and in the world that had shunned her the night she'd tried.

"Okay then."

"I love you, Austin."

"I see I was right about the little whore."

Callie froze.

No. Fucking. Way.

There was no way Morgan's mother could be in Montgomery Ink. There was no way she'd call Callie a whore.

Again.

Callie turned, but Austin didn't let go of her.

"Ms. McAllister."

"You bitch. You think you can pull my son away from me? You're nothing but a dirty tramp who thinks she can have my money. Look at you. That dirty drawing all over you and you're now humping some felon in broad daylight. Wait until I tell my son about your slutty ways."

"Excuse me? Who the *hell* do you think you are?" Maya stood up, glaring.

Callie closed her eyes and counted to ten. When she opened them, Sloane, Maya, Austin, Sloane's and Maya's clients, and Hailey—who must have come out of her café—stood in front of her.

They were all yelling, calling each other names and making the situation worse. No, she didn't want to crawl into a hole and die, but she wanted this to be the end of it. Morgan was worth a lot to her, but he had to get a handle on his mother.

For fuck's sake.

"Stop it. All of you."

No one listened.

She pushed her way through and snarled. "Let me handle this. I'm a big girl." She took a deep breath. Calling this woman a bitch and punching her in the face wouldn't help the situation. As much as it would make her feel better, she needed to talk with Morgan first. She wanted a future with him and going to jail for beating his mother up might hurt that.

So she'd stay calm.

For now.

Her friends quieted, but they didn't move. The woman opened her mouth to speak but Callie held up a hand.

"No. You've had your say. This is a place of business and the owners are behind me. You say anything else, and it's well within their rights to kick you out. I know you don't like me, but you need to go. Morgan is an adult and you need to let him make his own choices."

"You mean his mistakes."

Ouch.

"Goodbye."

"This isn't the end of this," she snapped then stormed out.

No, Callie didn't think it would be the end of it, but she needed to recover from the words that hurt more than they should have.

"What the fuck, Callie?" Maya shouted. "Why didn't you stand up for yourself?"

People started shouting at her and she closed her eyes, rubbing her temples. An arm came around her and she turned to see Hailey.

"Shut up. All of you," Hailey said softly.

Surprisingly they did.

"Now, let Callie speak and then we can get back to our own lives and let her be. Got it?"

Everyone nodded at Callie's friend and she relaxed.

"I didn't yell or hit her because it wouldn't have helped. She has an opinion of me I can't change. What I can do is talk to Morgan about it when I get to his place tonight. I won't let this happen again. I won't stand by and let her treat me like that. But I *will* talk to Morgan about it so I can find a way to go about this without fucking everything up."

"You really love this guy?" Austin asked softly.

"*This guy* is your friend." She let out a breath. "And yes. I love him. He doesn't know and frankly, I'm not ready to tell him. However, I *will* figure out what to do about his mother because this can't happen again. And I won't hold back again."

"Good, Callie," Sloane said. "Good. Because if she comes in again, I'm calling the cops so Maya doesn't beat the shit out of her."

They hugged her and she felt like she had a family rallying around her. The fact she had to have anyone do that at all worried her and she was really upset, but she pushed it aside. She'd finish her day, finish her next client, and then see Morgan at his house as planned.

His mother couldn't push her away, not when she felt like Morgan cared for her.

She just hoped it was enough.

****

Morgan ran a hand over his head and looked down at the box on his bed. He'd bought the diamond necklace that would serve as a day collar from an antique dealer, but now he worried he should have bought something new.

Unique.

Callie liked to wear older, previously cherished things and make them her own, so the idea that she might wear this as a collar that showed the world she was his made sense to him at the time.

He just hoped it still did.

They hadn't been together long, but the connection he felt couldn't be denied. He didn't want the twenty-four/seven life and he knew Callie didn't want it either. However, he wanted to know that she would be his and have her know that he would be there for no matter what. He wasn't getting any younger and he was old enough to know his own mind, what his heart wanted.

And they both wanted Callie.

He'd thought about an engagement ring, and for some reason, held back. Having a collar that she could wear in public that only a lucky few would understand the meaning of felt like a bigger step to him. Once they were both ready, he'd ask her to marry him so the rest of the world would know they belonged to each other.

It was Saturday so he had the day off of work and instead of finding other things he could be doing in terms of paperwork or client meetings, he shopped for the woman he loved.

Loved.

Hell, how had he fallen in love so fast? He wasn't the most romantic type, nor was he close to his feelings, but he couldn't deny what he felt for his Callie.

He wanted a future with the woman who on the outside looked to be the exact wrong thing for him. Appearances didn't matter to him and once he had her by his side, he'd kick those who dared voice objections to the curb. He knew his mother and sisters would be a problem, but they weren't living his life. His sisters might get over it, but his mother would always be an issue. She'd never find the one he chose good enough unless she orchestrated the match. Considering the women his mother had paraded around him before, he had no doubt that he wouldn't have been happy if he'd given in.

He'd hated himself for giving in to a single date with Heather. Although if he hadn't gone along with the plan, he might not have seen Callie again until she worked on his ink. Things wouldn't have been the same, and he might not have ever had the chance to experience the best thing in his life. He had to be grateful for the twists and turns of fate and know that he'd been there to find Callie for a reason.

Now he had her and he never wanted to let her go.

His fingers traced the jewels and lines of the collar.

He just hoped she accepted.

It could be too soon, but Morgan didn't think so. She was young, but had an old soul. Call it cliché, but he knew that soul and wanted to know more. He wanted to be her Dom, her mate, her one and only. He wanted her in his life until the day he took his last breath.

She'd accept him.

She had to.

Someone knocked on his door sharply and he frowned. Callie didn't have a key—yet—but she normally didn't knock so loudly. Maybe it was a neighbor. He put the collar in his dresser drawer and slid his hands down his shirt, preparing himself.

He took a deep breath.

This could be it.

He was so fucking nervous, it was funny, but he couldn't wait to see her face when he pledged himself to her.

He made his way to the door and opened it, the smile on his face falling when he saw his mother and Heather in the doorway.

"Home on a Saturday when you should be golfing or out to lunch with clients," his mother snapped as she pushed her way into his home. He was so startled she was even there, he let them in. "You're ruining your father's memory by being lazy and I won't have it. You hear me? I won't have you shaming me. Shaming the family."

Morgan took a deep breath and turned around to look at his mother and her guest. He didn't bother closing the door because he didn't want them to think they were welcome. He'd give them a minute or two then he'd kick them out. He was done with this. Done with letting his mother think she ruled his life and that she had any say in what he did or how he lived.

"If you're here to belittle me and judge what I do, you can walk right out that door. I'm done with you and your vitriol."

His mother narrowed her eyes. "Is it that tramp doing this to do you? That skank porn star."

Morgan ground his teeth. "Watch your mouth. You call Callie another name, I won't be responsible for my actions."

"You're wasting your life with her. If you really wanted to have sex with a whore, you could buy one. Heather wouldn't mind once you're married for a respectable amount of time and an heir on the way."

Morgan glanced at Heather who, of all things, nodded eagerly by his mother's side.

Dear God. There were two of them.

"You know what? Fuck you. Fuck you both."

His mother sucked in a breath. "Morgan," she gasped.

"Oh shut up. I'm the sole heir. You're the one who wanted to keep up with this sexist dynasty, then whatever. I own the trust. I own the family name. I'm the one with the power because you and Father are the ones who gave it to me." He'd change things for him and Callie, but he didn't say that then. "You can go to hell. I won't give you a dime. You can stay in your little home and hold onto what you have but you're not getting one fucking cent from me."

His mother paled, but didn't back down. "You can't do this to me. You won't be happy with that whore. You need Heather. She's the one who will help you advance yourself and your legacy."

"I refuse to hit a woman, so you better get out of my sight. Right. Now."

"Heather is the woman who can provide the heirs you need. Provide the life you've grown accustomed to."

This woman didn't understand a single thing coming out of his mouth. No matter what he did, she'd never understand. He was done with this.

"I've only ever wanted you to have what you deserve," his mother said sharply.

Or what she thought was best.

"You've paraded women around me for years." Heather came closer and he fisted his hands. "Callie isn't like Heather. She isn't like the others."

If he had been faster, he'd have stopped her. As it was, Heather threw her arms around him, pressing her lips to his.

He pushed her away quickly, wiping his mouth. "What the ever-loving *fuck*?"

"That's what you've been missing." She smirked, looked over his shoulder and he turned around.

Callie stood in the doorway, pale and trembling.

What had she heard? What had she seen?

From the look on her face, whatever it was hadn't been good.

"Callie..."

She held up her hand. "No. I see I'm interrupting."

She turned and ran down the path. He ached to follow her, but he had to get something settled once and for all.

He turned back to his mother and Heather. "Get. The. Fuck. Out." Morgan's voice was low and calm, alarmingly so. "We're done. I never want to see you again. You come near me, I call the cops. And won't your society friends just love hearing about that? Either of you come near me or Callie, and I will finish you."

He pulled his mother and Heather by the arms and pushed them out of the house. They screeched, but he didn't fucking care. He took a deep breath then grabbed his keys and prayed Callie hadn't left the driveway yet.

He might have just ruined the best thing in his life and he wasn't about to back away. He loved Callie Masters and he would not allow anything to come between them.

CHAPTER TEN

Callie's not like Heather. Not like the others.

That kiss.

That fucking kiss.

She'd seen the way Morgan's hands rested on Heather's hips. He might have pushed her away, but it hadn't been quick enough for her taste. Maybe Heather had thrown herself at him, but Callie had heard Morgan compare herself to the other woman who had come before her.

She always knew she was different than the others but she thought Morgan was stronger than what society demanded of him. Now she sat in her car, her hands shaking as she tried to turn on the ignition. If she didn't leave soon, she'd have to face Morgan again. There was no way he'd just let her go, he was too demanding for that.

Well, at least some part of her hoped for that. Call her jaded, crazy, and sick. Because that's what she was. Tears slid down her face and she cursed herself. She wouldn't cry over a man. She was better than that. So what if Morgan didn't think she was as good as the other woman who had been in his life.

So fucking what.

She knew she was the tattooed freak who was too young for him. She'd seen the evidence when she met him at the gala. Like a leopard, there was no changing her spots and she'd be damned if she'd force herself to try.

The knock on the window made her jump, but she refused to look over. The door opened and she cursed herself yet again for not locking it.

"Callie, baby. Come back inside. Let's talk."

She gripped the steering wheel, her gaze on her hands. "We have nothing to talk about, Morgan." Her voice broke and she swallowed hard. "I'm leaving so please shut the door."

"It wasn't what you think."

God. *That* line. Why did men think it was okay to use that line? He stood there acting like nothing was wrong when she was breaking inside. Breaking like the fragile woman she'd refused to be.

"Go away."

"Baby. Please come inside. It wasn't like that."

"I don't care what it was like. I'm going. Please close the door before I drive off with it open." This was all too much.

"Callie Masters. Stay," he ordered.

How. Dare. He.

He only ordered her to things in the bedroom. He had no fucking right to do it here. She turned to him, ignoring the pain in his eyes, the hard line of his jaw.

"I'm not your whore. You don't get to tell me what to do."

He looked as if she'd struck him and backed away. Her heart shattered, she closed the door, started the engine, and peeled out of the driveway. She knew it wouldn't be safe to drive too long, so she made it as far as Maya's house and stopped in front of it.

Had she overreacted?

Maybe.

Had she let her insecurities take over?

Possibly.

Had another woman kissed him?

Yes.

Had he said she wasn't as good as the others in his life?

Yes.

There wasn't another option for her.

Callie looked up as she finally turned off the car and saw Maya standing on her porch, a frown on her face. Still shaky, Callie got out of the car and Maya cursed.

"What happened? Who do I need to kill?"

Callie sputtered out a laugh that turned into a sob. "This is why I love you."

Maya held out her arms and Callie sank into the other woman. "Is it Morgan?" she asked as she led Callie into the house.

Callie nodded, trying to stop her tears. Damn it. She didn't want to cry. She wanted to be stronger than that, but it wasn't about to happen. At least not right then.

They sat on the couch and Callie told Maya everything. From the night at the gala, to the way Morgan had blended into her world—or so she'd thought—to what she'd seen when she walked in. All the while, Maya ran her hands down Callie's back, nodding or cursing softly.

"I'm sorry you had to deal with other people's negativity, baby. What they think means nothing. Their opinions aren't founded in anything but intolerance and cruelty. Morgan would have been damn lucky to have you. The fact he couldn't see that means he's not worth your time."

Callie winced, thinking over exactly what happened. "He pushed the other woman away when she kissed him."

"And he tried to use his dominance in the bedroom to force you to stay. That's not cool."

She shook her head. No, it hadn't been. Though he was always more dominant than her, he always gave her a choice when it mattered.

"Maybe I should have let him explain," she whispered.

Maya growled. "You can. Just because you left him so you could think, doesn't mean it's over. Unless that's what you need it to be. But you needed space to put everything together and he wasn't giving that to you."

She swallowed hard. She didn't know what she was going to do, but the vision of Heather's lips on his and the comparison he'd made hurt. Maybe in time she'd forgive, but right then, she couldn't face him.

"If you want, I can get my brothers to beat him up," Maya said softly.

Callie snorted.

"Wait," Maya said. "Fuck that. Let's do it ourselves."

Callie threw her head back and laughed, warmth filling the empty ache she hadn't known was there. It wouldn't fill completely, but her friend next to her helped. At least for a little while.

The next day Callie rolled her shoulders and opened her door to the woman she had a feeling would stop by sooner or later.

"Ms. McAllister."

The woman gave her a pinched look and moved to enter Callie's home. Oh no, that wouldn't do. She wasn't afraid any longer. She wouldn't be allowing this woman to walk all over her again. How this woman had figured out where Callie lived escaped her, but money and connections probably had something to do with it.

"You can stand out on the porch if you'd like to speak with me, but you're not welcome in my home."

Morgan's mother lifted her lip in disdain. "Like I'd want to step foot in this hovel."

Sure, honey. Save face. Whatever.

"What can I do for you?" See? She could be polite.

The other woman lifted her chin. "I wanted to find your price."

Callie blinked. "What?"

The woman smiled, but it wasn't a nice smile. "I want to know how much money you want to stay away from Morgan. I'm sure we can come up with an agreeable figure to keep you out of our lives."

Oh sweet Jesus, how little this woman knew.

"First off, honey, you can't pay me to keep out of his life." She was doing just fine on that account on her own, but she wasn't about to tell this bitch. "Second, if you really think money is the only way to get things done, you're sadly mistaken."

"You're just a little nobody who thinks she can weasel her way into our lives. I will not permit that."

She was done. So fucking done.

"I'm not a nobody. I'm Callie fucking Masters. I'm a talented artist. I have a job. I own my home. I have friends and family who love me. I'm not a dried up old prune who waves money around to save a legacy that doesn't belong to her. Shut up," she snapped when the woman opened her mouth to speak. "This is my property and my time to speak. I want nothing to do with you. My relationship has nothing to do with you." And it wouldn't damn it. Why had she let this woman's actions hurt her? She'd been hurt, but she'd hurt Morgan at the same time.

Fuck.

"You're a leech."

"No, honey. You are." With that, Callie stepped back and slammed the door in Morgan's mother's face.

That felt oddly amazing. She ran a hand up and down her arms, her skin tingling. She'd stood up for herself like she should have done in the first place. No, she hadn't kept anything from Morgan, but she hadn't been as forceful and honest to those in his life who had tried to keep them apart. She'd hidden herself to protect a relationship that wouldn't have lasted if she'd kept things from him.

Callie ran her hands through her hair and went to her notepad. She would draw to keep her mind off the agony in her heart. As she turned the pages, she passed the sketches she'd made for Morgan and she bit her lip. Damn it. Instead of tearing them out like she should have, she quickly passed them and found herself a blank page.

A blank page—just like how her future would be.

No, that wasn't right. She didn't have a blank page. She had friends and family who loved her, a job she couldn't wait to get back to, and dreams she wouldn't give up.

She just wouldn't have Morgan by her side.

Someone knocked on the door again and Callie ground her teeth. That fucking old lady.

She swung it open, not bothering to look before opening her mouth to speak.

"I told you to get the fuck out of here." She froze as she looked up at a haggard Morgan. He hadn't shaved and he wore the same clothes she'd seen him in the night before. Oh damn. It looked as if he'd had a worse night than she did.

Why were they doing this to each other?

"I'm not going, Callie. Not until you listen."

She swallowed hard. "I...I thought you were someone else."

He cocked his head. "Who else would you yell at to leave?"

She shrugged. No use in lying and keeping secrets. "Your mother."

Red tinged his cheeks and he cursed. "I'm sorry about that. I kicked her out of my home and my life, but she's not going down easy. On Monday, once she realizes the purse strings are officially gone, she'll back off."

Callie's eyes widened and she stepped back, letting him in so she could close the door. "You cut your mother off?"

Morgan cupped her face and she sighed. "Yes. I was in the process of doing that when you walked in."

She pulled away at the reminder. "You mean when you said I wasn't good enough and then let that woman kiss you?"

His eyes widened. "What the hell? I did *not* say that."

"Yes. Yes you did."

He shook his head and reached for her hand but she pulled away. "I said you weren't like the others. Meaning you're it for me Callie girl. The others that my mother wanted me to be with were vapid and shallow. They were nothing to me other than a nuisance. I tried to be a nice guy and let them down easily so as not to come across as a fucking bastard, but they wanted me for my name and money. You aren't them, baby girl. You're way out of their league. I'm so fucking sorry you thought different. Fuck. I'm sorry that you felt anything other than my love for you. I shouldn't have put you in a position where you could be hurt. I'm the one who is supposed to protect you and I let you get hurt. *I* hurt you."

Callie blinked up at him. "I...I don't understand." He reached out and cupped her face. This time she let him.

"I love you Callie Masters. I want to be with you until the last breath leaves my body. You're it for me. I shouldn't have let you walk out of the house yesterday, nor should I have ordered you to stay. I should have made it clear that you're the one I want in my life, my heart, my soul."

Tears slid down her cheeks, but she couldn't speak. Not yet.

"There may be those who think I'm too damn old for you, but I don't care. Fuck what anyone says because you're my forever, Callie. You're the one I want by my side through bad times and good. I want you to wear my collar every day and know that I will be your lover, your protector, and your heart, until the day I die. I want to know that you're mine. I want you forever, Callie girl."

He took the diamond necklace out of his pocket and she gasped. "One day I will ask you to marry me. One day I will get down on one knee so the world knows that you're mine as I'm yours. One day I will watch you grow round with our child and raise our precious babies by your side. For now, I want you to wear my collar and know that I will always be there for you. No matter what world we live in, what things may come, by wearing this you will know that I will be yours as you're mine."

"Morgan..." She couldn't speak. Her throat was closing and yet this was the happiest she'd ever felt in her life. Oh damn how she'd been wrong.

"Talk to me, Callie."

She sucked in a breath and placed her hand on his chest. "I love you too, Morgan. I love you with every ounce of my being. I know it's soon and we have time to grow and tangle with one another, but right now, I know that I love you. I can't wait for the day that I'm your wife, mother of your children and the fact that you know that I want time before that happens tells me that you love me more than I could ever know." She kissed his chest. Once. Twice. "I would be honored to wear your collar, to be yours," she whispered.

Morgan's hand wrapped around the back of her neck so his thumb still ran over her jaw. "Callie, this is the last time I will *ask* you to kneel. Will you kneel before me so I can place my collar on you? So you will know that I am your protector, your strength, your lover, just as you are my lover, my sanctuary, and the keeper of my heart."

She nodded and knelt before him, her body shaking. He moved her hair out of the way and placed the collar around her neck, clasping it with steady hands.

Steady.

He was her rock, her strength.

Thank God.

He held out his hand and she took it, standing up so she faced him. "I love you. I love the way you look with my mark on you." He cupped her face and kissed her. She put her soul into the kiss, deepening it so she could show him how much he meant to her, how much she wanted this and a future.

"You're mine, Callie. Always and forever."

She ran her hands down his chest, his body. "I love you, Morgan. I...you're it for me. I never thought it would happen and yet I can't imagine anything else."

He kissed her cheeks, her lips, her temples. "I'm sorry I made you cry. I will do everything in my power to make it up to you, to show you that you're it for me."

She met his gaze and licked her lips. "I know it, Morgan. We're not through and I know we have more to learn, more ways to grow, but I can't wait to do it by your side." She grinned then traced her hands over his back.

"I'm going to finish your ink, make you shine, then love you until the day I die."

He smiled back and she fell just that much more in love. "I'll be your everything. Your strength, your canvas, just yours."

Forever.

Next in the Montgomery Ink Series: Tempting Boundaries

A Note from Carrie Ann

Thank you so much for reading **Forever Ink**. I do hope if you liked this story, that you would please leave a review. Not only does a review spread the word to other readers, they let us authors know if you'd like to see more stories like this from us. I love hearing from readers and talking to them when I can. If you want to make sure you know what's coming next from me, you can sign up for my newsletter at www.CarrieAnnRyan.com; follow me on twitter at @CarrieAnnRyan, or like my Facebook page. I also have a Facebook Fan Club where we have trivia, chats, and other goodies. You guys are the reason I get to do what I do and I thank you.

Make sure you're signed up for my MAILING LIST so you can know when the next releases are available as well as find giveaways and FREE READS.

Forever Ink is a novella in the Montgomery Ink series! The first book, *Delicate Ink*, is out now! The next full-length book will be called *Tempting Boundaries* and is about Decker and Miranda. Those two have a long road ahead and I for one can't wait. I love Best Friend's Little Sister stories!

If you don't want to wait for more Montgomery Ink books, I also have my Redwood Pack, Talon Pack, and Dante's Circle series going in full swing now so there's always a Carrie Ann book on the horizon!

Thank you so much for going on this journey with me and I do hope you enjoyed my Montgomery Ink series. Without you readers, I wouldn't be where I am today.

Thank you again for reading and I do hope to see you again.

Carrie Ann

About this Author

New York Times and USA Today Bestselling Author Carrie Ann Ryan never thought she'd be a writer. Not really. No, she loved math and science and even went on to graduate school in chemistry. Yes, she read as a kid and devoured teen fiction and Harry Potter, but it wasn't until someone handed her a romance book in her late teens that she realized that there was something out there just for her. When another author suggested she use the voices in her head for good and not evil, The Redwood Pack and all her other stories were born.

Carrie Ann is a bestselling author of over twenty novels and novellas and has so much more on her mind (and on her spreadsheets *grins*) that she isn't planning on giving up her dream anytime soon.

www.CarrieAnnRyan.com

Also from this Author

His Choice
Tangled Innocence

Holiday, Montana Series:
Charmed Spirits
Santa's Executive
Finding Abigail
Her Lucky Love
Dreams of Ivory

Montgomery Ink:
Ink Inspired
Ink Reunited
Delicate Ink
Forever Ink (also found in Hot Ink)
Tempting Boundaries

Coming Soon:

Redwood Pack
Wicked Wolf

Talon Pack (Part of the Redwood Pack World)
Tattered Loyalties

Dante's Circle:
Fierce Enchantment

Montgomery Ink:
Harder than Words

Tempting Signs:
Finally Found You

Excerpt: Tempting Boundaries

Did you enjoy this selection? Why not try another romance from Fated Desires?

From New York Times Bestselling Author Carrie Ann Ryan's Montgomery Ink

There was just something about the scent of a grill, the feel of a cold beer in his hand, and the company of a family that truly loved him that made Decker Kendrick want to relax after a long day's work. If he added in the fact that he could go home and have the woman at his side under him, over him, and all around him, it would be a pretty fantastic way to end the day.

Colleen, his date to the Montgomery family barbeque and engagement party, leaned into him and batted her false eyelashes. He had no idea why she wore them. He thought she looked decent without them. But whatever—it was her body to fake up any way she wanted to. He'd been seeing Colleen off and on for a few months, more often in the past month since he'd called her up, hoping to get his mind off a certain long-legged brunette he shouldn't be thinking about in the first place.

The woman in question hadn't shown up to the party yet, and Decker was grateful. Hard to ignore her and keep her off his mind if she kept popping up everywhere he went. Though that wasn't really fair considering she was part of his family.

More like *he* was part of hers.

He was an honorary Montgomery, and she was the little sister.

Totally not for him.

"Decker? Baby?"

He blinked and looked down at Colleen. Not the woman who haunted his dreams and kept him up late at night. Jesus, he was a bad man. A very, very bad man. Sure, he was keeping it casual with Colleen—something she'd put on the table to begin with—but he shouldn't be thinking about a woman with long legs he couldn't have when he was here with someone else.

That wasn't the kind of guy he wanted to be.

"Colleen?" he answered back, keeping his voice low. He didn't normally bring dates to the Montgomery family gatherings, and as such, he didn't want everyone to hear everything he said. They were all nosy in the we-are-family-and-we-can-be-nosy-if-want-to sort of way, and he'd learned to deal with it. He hadn't planned on bringing her at all, but when she'd called to ask him to dinner, he'd mentioned he had plans, and she'd sort of invited herself along. It hadn't bothered him too much then, but now he felt kind of like an awkward ass about it. Since this was the first time he'd brought Colleen to any type of function with the Montgomerys, he'd been prepared to have the family question the two of them until they pecked them to death.

So far, that hadn't happened, and frankly, that was more telling about what the others in his life thought of the relationship. Their politeness and lack of prodding meant they didn't see a future. Considering Colleen hadn't wanted a future to begin with when it came to her and Decker, that was just fine with him. He didn't see himself marrying the woman anyway. They were friends. Sort of.

"You're thinking too hard." She rubbed the little spot between his eyebrows, and he frowned. She wasn't usually so touchy-feely or attentive. Weird.

He pulled back, uncomfortable with the display of affection—or whatever it was—in front of the family that had taken him in so long ago.

"Just tired. Hauling a total of a half-ton of porcelain up and down stairs all day makes for a long workday. We also punched out our other project the day before. So I'm ready for a nap. Or another beer."

She wrinkled her nose, probably at the mention of his work. Another reason he'd never get too serious with her. She hated the fact he was a blue-collar worker and not some suit-wearing businessman who could keep her in diamonds and silks. She worked her butt off at her job and wore the expensive clothes that came with her world. That wasn't something he wanted in the long run. He worked for Montgomery Inc., the construction arm of the family businesses. He was the project manager right under Wes and Storm, the Montgomery twins who had taken over the family business when their parents, Harry and Marie, retired.

Wes was the OCD planner of the company and got his hands dirty daily with the bump and grind that came with being one of the top privately owned construction companies in Denver. Storm was the lead architect and a genius when it came to finding the right flow for a refurbished building or how to start from scratch with a piece of land that could be used carefully.

Decker had started out as a teenager working under Harry doing every kind of grunt work he could get his hands on. He'd gone to college only because the Montgomery twins had, as had his best friend, Griffin—another Montgomery—and because the state had helped him out. He wouldn't have been able to afford it otherwise. He'd gone to the local university, busted his ass for his degree, then went right back to working for the family that had raised him when his own blood family had failed.

He ground his teeth.

Best not think about the others right then. Not if he wanted to stay civil—he looked down at the beer in his hand—and sober.

"Must you talk about those matters with me?" Colleen asked, breaking through his thoughts.

He shrugged. He honestly didn't know why he'd brought her that evening other than because he was in a rut, and he hadn't thought to say no. They liked each other well enough, but they weren't in love. He hadn't slept with her in months either. Despite the fact that his balls were so blue from lack of sex—his right hand could only do so much—he hadn't wanted to sleep with one woman when his mind was on the other. Sure, he'd been trying to date to get those thoughts out of his head, but he wasn't about to use another woman fully like that.

"I work with everything that goes in a house or building," Decker said, his voice low. He had a deep, growly voice according to the-woman-who-shall-not-be-named, and when he got annoyed or emotional, his voice just got deeper.

Colleen didn't care for it.

"Yes, dear, but you don't have to talk about it." She raised her chin and looked out at the yard. He'd helped with the initial landscaping years ago when he was trying to find his place within the business. He'd been better at digging the holes and lifting bags of mulch, rather than doing the actual planning. Marie was the brains behind that. She'd told them what to do, and he and her boys had hopped to it.

In the end, the place looked great with tons of vegetation that looked as though it was natural, rather than lines and perfectly square things that made no sense.

"Did you hear me, Decker? What is going on with you? I said don't talk about things like that, not to stop talking at all."

He barely resisted the urge to roll his eyes. "Sorry to bother you," he mumbled, not sorry in the least. "Why don't you go talk to, uh, the girls over there while I get another drink?" He couldn't remember the two girls who worked with Sierra, the newly engaged woman and star of the party, but they seemed to get along with anyone. Hopefully, they'd make friends with Coleen so this evening wouldn't be a total waste.

She raised a brow and looked pointedly at his hand. Seriously? Jesus Christ. He shouldn't have brought her here. Or rather, he shouldn't have let her invite herself in the first place. She didn't belong, and he didn't know why he was kidding himself by trying to make it work when neither of them truly wanted it.

"I've had one beer, and I'll have one more since we have a couple hours left. I won't drink more than that." He wouldn't have had to explain himself to the Montgomerys. They knew enough about where he'd come from that him getting behind the wheel, even slightly buzzed, wasn't an option.

"If you say so," she clipped then strutted off to the girls on the other side of the backyard.

His shoulders relaxed marginally, and he cursed himself for it. He *liked* Coleen. He really did. She wasn't a bad person. She just didn't understand him.

Whose fault is that?

It wasn't like he'd told her all that much about himself, and he'd never once mentioned his past.

"Shit, bro, you look like you ate something rotten," Wes said as he walked toward him. He had the Montgomery blue eyes and chestnut hair, only his was neatly clipped and worked with his OCD persona.

Storm, Wes's twin, walked beside him. While Wes was a bit lanky, Storm had more of a build on him. He was also a bit more rugged with his shaggy hair, light beard, and flannel shirt over another light shirt, while Wes had his button-up shirt over nice jeans. It never made any sense to Decker that the twin who worked with his hands more often than not as the other general contractor preferred dressier clothes on his day off while the twin who sat behind his desk drawing when he wasn't in the field wore more rugged clothes. Well, considering each of them worked side by side with Decker and sweated their asses off regularly, it didn't matter what they wore now, as long as they worked hard during the day.

Which they did.

"Bro?" Decker asked, a smile on his face. "You working with the kids at Austin's shop now?" Austin was the oldest Montgomery and owned half of Montgomery Ink, the tattoo shop side of the family business, with their sister, Maya. It was also Austin and Sierra's engagement party and the reason they were all at the barbecue that evening.

Storm snorted. "We say bro sometimes. Doesn't make us some college kids who want bad ink."

"I don't do bad ink, asshole," Maya snapped as she came up to them. She wrapped her arm around Decker's middle, and he hugged her back. Why couldn't he be this comfortable around *all* the Montgomery women?

She pulled back before he could squeeze her tighter. Maya liked her space, and Decker liked her all the more for it. Her dark brown bangs were severe across her forehead, and she'd done a weird eyeliner thing that made her look like some fifties rocker pin-up. The red lipstick just made her look like she'd smile at you—then kick you in the ass.

"I meant that he wants bad ink because he doesn't know what good ink is," Storm said, backtracking. Wes and Storm might be the second oldest in the family, but no one messed with Maya and walked away without a limp. "Not that you give bad ink."

Wes laughed then shut up as Maya glared.

Decker, being the smart one of the group, kept his face neutral.

Maya narrowed her eyes at the three of them then nodded. "Okay, so tell me what's going on. Jake couldn't make it today, and I'm bored."

"When are you just going to admit that Jake is your boyfriend?" Wes asked.

Decker closed his eyes. It was like the twins *wanted* to die by her hand tonight.

"He's not my fucking boyfriend," Maya growled then lifted her chin, speaking softer this time. "He's my friend. I don't know why a guy and a girl can't just be friends without the rest of the world wondering if they're fucking."

Decker raised a brow then looked at the space between them.

Maya waved him off. "You're a brother, not a friend. So the world wouldn't ever think you'd be fucking a Montgomery girl. That'd be all kinds of wrong."

He swallowed hard and tried to keep the frown off his face. Shit. She was right. No one would think he'd ever be with a Montgomery girl. Maya was like his sister, as was Meghan, the eldest girl. Meghan was even married to an asshole, but married just the same.

Miranda though...Miranda was his best friend's little sister and had welcomed him into her family to boot.

There was no way he could ever think of her as more.

Or rather, he should *stop* thinking about her as possibly more.

"Anyway," Wes continued, "we came over here to ask what's up with Decker. He looked like he stepped in shit or something."

Decker rolled his eyes. Wes really liked making things sound worse than they were. "I'm fine. Just a long day." He rolled his shoulders, and the twins did the same. They'd hauled right by his side, and he knew they ached just as much.

"Tell me about it," Storm grumbled. "I never want to look at another toilet again."

"Charming," Maya said dryly.

"So, have you found a new receptionist yet?" Decker asked Maya, changing the subject from toilets to the running joke of the family. The shop had been through four or five receptionists this year alone. They had fantastic artists and had even just promoted their apprentice, Callie, to full time. However, they couldn't keep a receptionist to save their lives. The college kids always left for greener pastures, and the other ones thought it was fun to come in high around pointy needles. It might be legal to smoke, but that didn't mean they wanted their staff lit up while working.

"You can't have Tabby," Wes put it. "She's ours." Tabby was the Montgomery Inc. receptionist and a goddess with organization. She and Wes were a team in OCD heaven.

Maya cursed under her breath. "I don't want Tabby. She'd color code my ink in a weird way, and then I wouldn't want to move anything around. And no, we haven't found a receptionist. I don't know what it is. This latest guy just wanted free ink. Free. I pay for my own tattoos, you know. I won't let Austin do it for free because his work is *worth* my money. Wanting it free in our place just shows disrespect."

Decker snorted. "At least you get the family discount." Maya looked over her shoulder and discreetly flipped him off.

Decker frowned since she tried to hide it then smiled as Meghan's kids, Cliff and Sasha, ran into the backyard, barreling toward their uncles on the other side of the yard. They'd be over here soon for sure to see the rest of them. He loved those damn kids.

"You get the discount too, brother mine," Maya said. "But the discount isn't all that much in the scheme of things. This idiot wanted it all for free. So he huffed away and found another shop most likely." She shrugged. "Not as good a shop as ours, but whatever."

"There's no shop as good as yours." He rubbed between his shoulder blades. "Speaking of, I need to make an appointment for the ink on my back." Maya's eyes brightened, and he cursed. "With Austin, hon. It's his turn." All of the Montgomerys took turns with the other siblings when it came to their ink. Both of them were talented, and picking one over the other was nearly impossible.

Besides, they both had nasty tempers if they didn't get to be part of the siblings' and parents' art.

"Fine. I see how it is. You like him better." She sniffed and wiped a non-existent tear at the edge of her eye. Not that she actually touched her makeup in the process, but the move worked for her.

Decker rolled his eyes then punched her softly in the shoulder. "Shut up. You *just* did work on my arm, and you get my leg next. It's Austin's turn now."

She smiled, and he wasn't sure if it was a good one or a *you'll be sorry* one, but he rolled with it.

He looked over his shoulder to see Colleen in a conversation with one of Sierra's girls so he let her be then looked at the empty beer bottle in his hand. "I'm going to get a refill. Any of you want something?"

They shook their heads, and he said his goodbyes before walking over to the cooler. Alex, another Montgomery—seriously, there were eight siblings and countless cousins so he was always walking over a Montgomery or two—stood by the cooler, a tumbler of amber liquid in his hand.

Decker looked over his shoulder at the crowd and frowned. "Where's Jessica?" Jessica was Alex's high school sweetheart and wife. When they'd first gotten married a few years ago, she'd always come to the family events, though she never exactly fit in. It wasn't like she tried, either. The Montgomerys had tried on their part to welcome her into their midst, but for some reason, it never really took. Now, come to think of it, Decker hadn't seen her at one of these events in awhile.

Alex snorted then took another drink. From the glassy look in his eyes, this wasn't his first drink.

Well fuck. This wasn't good.

"Like she'd come to one of these," Alex drawled. He didn't sound drunk, but Decker could never tell with Alex. The fact that he knew something was off at all was because of experience. He'd dealt with enough drunks and near-drunks to last a lifetime. "She's off with her girls at the spa or something. She didn't feel like celebrating Sierra and Austin's engagement since she's never actually met Sierra."

Decker's eyebrows lifted toward his hairline. "She hasn't met Sierra yet? How is that possible?" Jessica was already a Montgomery, and it wasn't like Sierra was new to the family. She already lived with Austin and was helping raise his son.

"It's possible when you're Jessica." Alex took another drink and looked the other way.

Okay then. Conversation over.

Decker shifted from foot to foot. Alex had always been the one to joke and make people laugh. That wasn't what Decker saw now, and it scared him a bit. The man in front of him looked angry...and drunk. Decker knew drunks. He'd lived with one off and on until he'd finally been able to break free.

He didn't want to see it again.

"You want a water, Alex?" he asked calmly. Tiptoeing around it wouldn't help, but coming right out and asking if the man he called his brother was an alcoholic wouldn't either.

Alex gave him a small smile instead of getting angry, which surprised Decker. "I'm good." The man didn't leave to refill his drink, but that didn't mean he wouldn't do it once Decker was out of sight. He didn't know what to do, but as long as Alex knew he was there, maybe that could help.

"Okay. Just...you know I'm here, right?" he asked softly.

Alex's face closed up, and he lifted his chin. Damn. "I'm good," he repeated.

Decker searched his face and couldn't find a way past the barriers. He'd keep an eye on him though. This man was his brother, blood or no.

He got a soda instead of a beer, his stomach not quite ready for booze after that, and walked over to his best friend, Griffin. The man held the same look as the rest of the Montgomerys, dark hair and blue eyes, but with the same slender build as Wes, rather than the brick-house look of Austin or even Storm. Griffin was the easiest going of the family, the writer who spent most of his time in his own head, rather than in the real world. His mess of a house reflected that, but Decker loved him anyway. They were the same age, so they'd grown up like twins after a while. Decker might have more in common with Austin on some levels and work closely with Wes and Storm, but Griffin was the one he knew best.

"Glad to see you finally found your way over to me," Griffin joked. He sat in one of the outdoor chairs and waved at the empty one. "Take a seat. I'm people watching."

Decker laughed then did as he was told. "First, you could have come over to me. It wasn't like I was blocking you. Second, this is your family. Why are you watching them?"

Griffin took a sip of his beer then shook his head. "You were with Colleen, and as I can't stand that giggle of hers, I didn't want to join in."

"Giggle?" Decker asked, a little annoyed that Grif would judge his date. It wasn't like he and Colleen were married, but still. Pointing out something like that didn't seem right.

"Giggle," Griffin repeated. "You know it. Whenever she giggles, your shoulders tense, and you get that little twitch at the corner of your mouth."

Huh, now that he mentioned it... Nope, not going to think about it. He still had the rest of the night and probably more nights with the woman. It wouldn't do to nitpick and then zoom in on those quirks for too long. He wouldn't be able to get over it.

"You noticed all that?" he asked, draining some of his soda.

"Yep. I told you. I people watch. In fact, I'm watching that asshole and my sister right now. I really want to beat the shit out of him, but I'm not sure she'd appreciate that. She doesn't like when the rest of us threaten to maim or murder her husband."

Decker frowned then looked over at Meghan and her husband, Richard. Meghan was three years older than him and had always struck him as warm, friendly, and not to be messed with. She was like the mother hen of the clan and stood up for herself.

But not now.

Now she had her shoulders slouched and her head down. Richard was snapping about something, and each time he spoke, Meghan turned in on herself just that much more. Nope. This wasn't going to do.

Decker stood up, set his soda down, and then rolled his shoulders. "You ready?" he growled at Griffin, who had stood with him. Like there was any other way to react when he saw someone he cared about being beaten down emotionally.

"Yep. Let's not beat the shit out of him since their kids are here, and it's Austin and Sierra's time, but yeah, I'm ready."

They stalked toward the couple, and Richard puffed out his chest as he noticed them. The man had once had a decent build and hair on his head. Now it looked like he was balding a bit, but he brushed it in just the right way that you couldn't tell unless you'd seen him before. He also had a little bit of a gut that came with lack of activity. Though he wore suits that shouted their worth, the effect was lost at the straining button on his stomach.

"What?" the bastard snapped.

Decker smiled, but it wasn't a nice one. He put his arm around Meghan, who stiffened. He let that pass and kept his arm on her. The more people who cared about her, the better.

"Just wanted to say hi to my sister, that's all," he said smoothly.

Richard scoffed. "She's not your sister. You're just the trash. Get your hands off my wife."

He didn't even wince at the word trash. He'd heard worse and usually from people who should have meant more to him than this sack of shit.

"Richard," Meghan admonished, her voice gaining strength. *Atta girl.* "Decker is family."

Decker squeezed her shoulders, but she didn't relax. Damn.

"She's right about that," Griffin said easily.

"Well then, wife, you're not a Montgomery anymore," Richard said, baring his teeth. "You'd do best to remember that. Go get the brats. We're leaving. We said our hellos to the happy couple—they won't be happy for long knowing the way that brute is—so it's time to go."

Why the fuck was Meghan still with this man? He treated her like shit and beat down on her emotionally. Decker didn't think Richard touched her with his fists, but one could never tell. Decker should know.

Flashes of meaty fists and breath tainted with cheap booze filled his mind, and he shook it off.

"Once a Montgomery, always a Montgomery," Griffin said from his side.

"Pretty much," Decker said smoothly. "If you're in a hurry, you can head out and we'll get Meghan and the kids home when they're ready to leave."

"She's *my* wife. Not yours."

"Decker. Griffin. Let it go," she whispered.

Decker shook his head. "Sorry, hon, Austin and Sierra's party just started, and we haven't done the toasts yet. You should stay. If Richard needs to go, he can go." He looked into her eyes and prayed she understood he meant more than for that one night.

"Fine. Keep the brats here."

"I need the boosters," Meghan whispered.

"Then you should come with me," Richard snapped.

Meghan glared. Good. There was still some fire in her. "I'm not risking my children's lives because you want to leave early."

"Our children, Meghan. You best remember that." He smiled coolly, and Decker froze.

So that's why she stayed. For the kids. That motherfucker.

"We got boosters in the house," Griffin said. "Mom and Dad keep them in case they have the kids." He didn't mention that Decker had bought them when Richard had left Meghan alone with the kids and taken her car one time.

She didn't need to remember that. On second thought, maybe she did.

"Fine." Richard didn't even say goodbye to Cliff and Sasha before stomping away. Meghan visibly relaxed when the man left.

"Meghan..." Decker started, but she held up a hand.

"No. Not here. I need to take care of my children."

He nodded, knowing she was stronger than his own mother. At least he hoped. "I'm here if you need me."

"Me too," Griffin added. "We all are."

She cupped both their cheeks and smiled sadly. "I know. I love you both. Now go and talk to Austin or Sierra or something. I need a moment."

Decker nodded before leaving her alone with Griffin. His friend would take care of her until she pushed him away because she thought she was too strong to lean on someone. He wouldn't let her situation grow to be what his past had been, but he also knew there was only so much a person could do without physically pulling them away.

That wouldn't help anyone.

"That prick gone?" Austin growled when Decker reached him. Sierra punched her fiancé in the stomach, and he winced before wrapping his arm around her.

"Watch your mouth," she whispered and looked over his shoulder.

Austin and Decker looked as well. Austin's son, Leif, stood near, his attention on whatever Storm was saying and not on Austin's words thankfully. Leif had come to the family after his mother had passed and Austin had found out he was a daddy. Strange as hell to think of it all, but Decker loved the boy like he'd been raised with them from birth. He fit right in.

"Yep. That prick is gone. I'm worried about her. Alex too." He might as well let it all out. Austin was his big brother, and Sierra was going to be a new sister. They were family.

Sierra shook her head. "We all are. They know we're here, and if there's anything we can do, we'll figure it out."

Decker pulled her from Austin's arms and gave her a tight hug before pressing his lips to hers in a hard kiss.

"Hey, get your mouth off my woman."

Decker pulled back and smiled at a flushed Sierra. "But she's such a pretty woman." He tucked her into his side. "See? She fits just right."

Austin growled then pulled a laughing Sierra to him. "No, she fits against my side. You're an ass."

Decker grinned. "A hot ass. And you know it."

"You two are idiots, but I love you." Sierra laughed at her words, but Austin growled. "I mean I love Decker in a brotherly sort of way. I love you in a sexy, sweaty way. Okay?"

Decker raised his hands in mock surrender. "I so do not need to think about that. I'm going to go see how Harry's doing. Let me know when you want help with your toast or something."

Austin nodded, but his eyes were all for Sierra.

Fuck, what would it be like to have a love like that? A person who was by your side no matter what.

Decker didn't think he'd ever have that. Not with the way his mind and body wanted the one person he couldn't have. In his experience, love didn't last, and marriages were only shackles he knew some people could never be rid of.

Of course, that wasn't quite true since the couple he'd just left seemed to be on the right path, but he wasn't sure yet. Then of course, the couple he was in front of had been together for over four decades and still looked like they were more in love every day.

But love hurt when one person was sick.

Harry Montgomery had always been larger than life. He was a big man with an even bigger heart. Yet the man in the chair in front of him didn't look like that now. The extracorporeal radiation therapy—Decker had been reading up—that targeted Harry's prostate cancer had taken a toll. The man looked so much smaller, weaker, and paler than Decker had ever seen.

The doctors told him they'd caught the cancer early and things were looking good, but the treatment looked like it hurt worse than the cancer. And now, in Decker's eyes, Marie was forced by love, duty and circumstance to stand by her husband's side as he grew weaker and weaker. How was that reward for love? How could that be worth it? The pain and loss that could come with growing close to someone didn't make sense to him, and he wasn't sure he deserved it in the first place.

"Come here, boy," Harry growled out, a sparkle in his eye.

Thank God.

Decker crouched near him, his hands shaking. He didn't know what to do. Did he hug him? It looked like, with just one hug, Decker would break the man he thought of as his father.

"How you feeling?" he asked. And damn if his voice hadn't choked up.

Harry patted his arm as Marie came to Decker's side, kneeling so she could hug him. He put his arm around her, inhaling that sweet Mom scent that had worked so well to calm him as a kid.

"I'm doing better," Harry said softly. "It doesn't look like it, but I'm not dying. Not yet."

Decker felt like he'd been stabbed in the heart with those words. Jesus. He couldn't lose Harry. He couldn't.

"Hey, don't look at me like that," Harry said. "I told you all I'd be honest with you about my recovery. We caught it early. The radiation hurts like a bitch, but we're pushing through. Now I wanted you to come over here because, one, you're my son and I wanted to see you, and two, because you helped with that prick of a husband my daughter chose. I couldn't get up to fix it, so thank you." The slight helplessness in Harry's eyes was too much.

Decker swallowed hard and willed his eyes not to fill with tears. Fuck.

"I'd have kicked his ass..." He shot a look at Marie. "I mean his butt, but the kids were there."

"You can say ass when it comes to Richard," Marie put in. "He *is* an ass."

Decker threw his head back and laughed. "I love you both. I just wanted to make sure you knew that."

Marie's eyes filled with tears. "Oh, that's the sweetest thing. The sweetest thing. We love you too, baby."

Harry nodded, and Decker leaned into the strong woman's arms.

The hairs on the back of his neck rose, and he stood up slowly. He turned to see Miranda walking into the backyard, her long legs bare under her sundress.

Holy fuck, she looked amazing.

He willed his cock not to fill, considering he was standing between her parents. Griffin came up to his side, and Decker knew there was a special place in hell for a man who lusted after his best friend's little sister.

Harry and Marie gave him a knowing look, and he held back a groan. Yep. He was going to hell. He was going to burn, and he'd deserve every moment of it.

Miranda turned to them and smiled brightly, her eyes twinkling.

He fought to keep his gaze on her face and not on her breasts or her legs that never quit.

He could do this.

This was Miranda Montgomery. The woman who was a girl no longer, and she was not for him.

He wouldn't drool over her. He wouldn't make an ass out of himself.

Griffin gave him a weird look, and Decker groaned inwardly.

Yep.
Going to hell.

An Alpha's Path

Did you enjoy this selection? Why not try another romance from Fated Desires?

From New York Times Bestselling Author Carrie Ann Ryan's Redwood Pack Series

Melanie is a twenty-five year old chemist who has spent all of her adult life slaving at school. With her PhD in hand, she's to start her dream job, but before she does, her friend persuades her to relax and try to live again. A blind date set up through her friends seems like the perfect solution. Melanie can take one night away from the lab and let her inner vixen out on a fixed blind date – a chance to get crazy with a perfect stranger. The gorgeous hunk she's to meet exceeds her wildest dreams – but he is more than what he appears and Melanie's analytical mind goes into overdrive.

Kade, a slightly older werewolf (at over one hundred years), needs a night way from the Pack. Too many responsibilities and one near miss with a potential mate made Kade hide in his work, the only peace he can find. His brother convinces him to meet the sexy woman for a one night of fun. What could it hurt? But when he finds this woman could be his mate, can he convince her to leave her orderly, sane world and be with him and his wolf-half, for life?

Dust of My Wings

Did you enjoy this selection? Why not try another romance from Fated Desires?

From New York Times Bestselling Author Carrie Ann Ryan's Dante's Circle Series

Humans aren't as alone as they choose to believe. Every human possesses a trait of supernatural that lays dormant within their genetic make-up. Centuries of diluting and breeding have allowed humans to think they are alone and untouched by magic. But what happens when something changes?

Neat freak lab tech, Lily Banner lives her life as any ordinary human. She's dedicated to her work and loves to hang out with her friends at Dante's Circle, their local bar. When she discovers a strange blue dust at work she meets a handsome stranger holding secrets – and maybe her heart. But after a close call with a thunderstorm, she may not be as ordinary as she thinks.

Shade Griffin is a warrior angel sent to Earth to protect the supernaturals' secrets. One problem, he can't stop leaving dust in odd places around town. Now he has to find every ounce of his dust and keep the presence of the supernatural a secret. But after a close encounter with a sexy lab tech and a lightning quick connection, his millennia old loyalties may shift and he could lose more than just his wings in the chaos.

Warning: Contains a sexy angel with a choice to make and a green-eyed lab tech who dreams of a dark-winged stranger. Oh yeah, and a shocking spark that's sure to leave them begging for more.

Charmed Spirits

Did you enjoy this selection? Why not try another romance from Fated Desires?

From New York Times Bestselling Author Carrie Ann Ryan's Holiday Montana Series

Jordan Cross has returned to Holiday, Montana after eleven long years to clear out her late aunt's house, put it on the market, and figure out what she wants to do with the rest of her life. Soon, she finds herself facing the town that turned its back on her because she was different. Because being labeled a witch in a small town didn't earn her many friends...especially when it wasn't a lie.

Matt Cooper has lived in Holiday his whole life. He's perfectly content being a bachelor alongside his four single brothers in a very small town. After all, the only woman he'd ever loved ran out on him without a goodbye. But now Jordan's back and just as bewitching as ever. Can they rekindle their romance with a town set against them?

Warning: Contains an intelligent, sexy witch with an attitude and drop-dead gorgeous man who likes to work with his hands, holds a secret that might scare someone, and really, *really*, likes table tops for certain activities. Enough said.

Made in the USA
Charleston, SC
21 April 2015